"At this point, no one is above suspicion."

"And you are investigating who the leak could be?" Holly asked eagerly. She put her hands on his shoulders, her face close to his. "Oh, Hunt, do let me help! Please?"

"Absolutely not!" He drew back, aghast. "That would be completely inappropriate, Holly, and possibly dangerous, as well."

"Are you not even trying to find out who it is?" Her expression was clouded.

"Of course I am," he said gently. "We all are. But very cautiously, through time-honoured means. 'Tis safest that way."

Holly sighed, apparently capitulating. But in the morning she had every intention of asking Noel to look into the matter for her. If she could discover the traitor's identity herself, her husband would have to realize how valuable a partner she could be.

Regency England: 1811-1820

"It was the best of times,
it was the worst of times...."

As George III languished in madness, the pampered and profligate Prince of Wales led the land in revelry and the elegant Beau Brummel set the style. Across the Channel, Napoleon continued to plot against the English until his final exile to St. Helena. Across the Atlantic, America renewed hostilities with an old adversary, declaring war on Britain in 1812. At home, Society glittered, love matches abounded and poets such as Lord Byron flourished. It was a time of heroes and villains, a time of unrelenting charm and gaiety, when entire fortunes were won or lost on a turn of the dice and reputation was all. A dazzling period that left its mark on two continents and whose very name became a byword for elegance and romance.

Books by Brenda Hiatt

HARLEQUIN REGENCY ROMANCE

A CHRISTMAS BRIDE

Brenda Hiatt

Harlequin Books

TORONTO • NEW YORK • LONDON
AMSTERDAM • PARIS • SYDNEY • HAMBURG
STOCKHOLM • ATHENS • TOKYO • MILAN
MADRID • WARSAW • BUDAPEST • AUCKLAND

For my friends on the GEnie RomEx,
who were of invaluable help on this book.
Thank you.

ISBN 0-373-31212-1

A CHRISTMAS BRIDE

PROLOGUE

July 1812

"OH, NOEL, can't I *please* come with you?" Holly seized her twin brother's coat sleeve and put on her most beguiling smile. "I'm as capable of heroics as you are, and two of us could be of twice as much help to England as one."

"We went over all this yesterday," said Noel firmly. "You promised to do your part here on English soil, covering for my absence."

"But I speak French as well as you do, thanks to Maman and Grand-père. We could be a team, just the way we used to be when we were younger. I would make a marvellous spy, Noel. You've said so yourself." Despite her eagerness Holly kept her voice low, even though the dusty village road was yet deserted in this cool hour before dawn.

"You've always been a marvel for sticking your nose where it don't belong," he admitted, "but that's not quite the same thing. Anyway, those were mere childhood games, Holly—this will be the genuine article." Noel's whisper was adamant. "We are nearly twenty now, you and I. France in wartime is no place for a young woman. I'll do far better alone, for Uncle Henri might well find me a clerk's position in Paris, where he could never find one for you. Besides, there is the matter of your come-out this fall. You'll scarce notice I am gone, I daresay, once you're caught up in the whirl of Society."

Holly snorted. "I never wished for a formal début, and well you know it. Blanche has always said the London ton are snobbish beyond belief."

"To her, I doubt not they were—fat, prissy, parading thing that she is." Noel's mouth twisted with disgust. "She must say something, you know, to account for the fact that she didn't take in three Seasons on the market. But you're different. I'd have insisted Maman fire you off last spring, had we not still been in mourning. But even during the Little Season, you'll likely nab yourself an earl at the very least!" His hazel eyes twinkled irrepressibly in the faint light of approaching sunrise.

In spite of the pain she felt at her brother's imminent departure, Holly had to chuckle at his absurdity. Her dowry was respectable, but scarcely enough to tempt a peer. "Merely an earl?" she asked with assumed lightness. "If I can't go off with you to become a national heroine, I shall look to become at least a marchioness, or perhaps even a duchess!"

"That's better," said Noel approvingly. Then he sobered. "Now remember, you are not to breathe a word to anyone—*anyone*—of where I am going. It could be extremely dangerous, especially since I'm not precisely 'official.' I will get word to you if I possibly can, using our old code, but as far as Maman and everyone else is concerned, I've joined a regiment taking ship for Upper Canada to defend it against the Americans."

Holly nodded solemnly. "I won't forget. But I *will* find some way to do my bit here, Noel, you'll see." Her voice caught as she heard the low rumble of the approaching stage. It rounded the curve and its pale lamps twinkled into view.

"Oh, *must* you go?" she cried suddenly, startling herself as much as her brother. "As a spy—especially an unofficial spy—you will be in far more danger than if you were truly going to fight as an officer. And whatever would I do if—"

"Ever my sentimental little raven," chuckled Noel, gently tugging his sister's straight ebony tresses, so unlike his own curly chestnut mop. "You of all people know how much I want to do this. And England needs me in this capacity, whether she knows it yet or not."

The stage pulled to a halt before them, the horses stamping and jingling their harnesses.

"Take care of Maman—and old Arrow, here." He patted the hound at her side. "Don't let Blanche ride roughshod over any of you."

Digging her fingernails into her palms, Holly forced a smile. "You will win the war for England, I know. But do be careful!" Blinking rapidly, Holly fought to hold back the tears that suddenly threatened. She was determined that her brother's last sight of home would not be of her weeping.

Noel gave her a quick, rough hug. "I promise. And you do your damnedest to catch yourself that marquess!"

His luggage was stowed and in less than a minute the coach was under way again. As the bobbing lamps receded, Holly's shoulders sagged and her tears, no longer held in check, ran freely down her cheeks.

CHAPTER ONE

Christmas Eve, 1812

"Do stop twitching, *chérie*," admonished Mrs. Paxton as she tried to adjust Holly's veil. "'Tis nearly time for you to go down."

In spite of her mother's remonstrances, Holly turned her head slightly, trying to get a peep at herself in the glass. "I know the bridegroom is not supposed to see me before the ceremony, Maman, but surely I may have a look at myself!"

"*Eh, bien.* You are ready, I think." Mrs. Paxton stepped back and allowed her daughter to turn completely around.

"'Tis a shame white does not suit you so well as it does me," said Blanche peevishly from her place by the window. She shook her head slightly to better admire, in a small hand mirror, the fall of her blond curls against the rose velvet bridesmaid's gown she was wearing for the occasion. Plainly, she had still not forgiven her younger sister for marrying out of turn.

Finally able to examine herself in the pier glass, Holly felt sure she had never looked so well, not even in her finest ball gown. Despite Blanche's words, she thought the white became her quite well, the lace over satin looking as sumptuous as it felt. Her black locks were swept up beneath the Brussels lace veil, and her green eyes positively glowed.

"Pray don't do anything to embarrass us, Holly," Blanche advised as their mother handed Holly the fragrant hothouse flowers she was to carry. "It is scandalous enough that you are marrying Vandover a mere two months after your betrothal—and in the wilds of Yorkshire instead of in London."

"Blanche, *mon ange,* do not add to our little bride's nervousness." Mrs. Paxton gave a quick shake of her head.

But Holly spoke up. "'Tis not scandalous at all. I think it very sweet that Lord Vandover wished to marry on my birthday. And, Blanche, you know that he insisted on holding the wedding here so that his grandmother would not miss it. The two of them are very close."

Holly could understand what was bothering Blanche. Not only was she marrying first, but she had attracted a peer. The thought of herself as a marchioness—and eventually, a duchess—seemed vaguely absurd even to Holly. For the hundredth time she wondered what the dashing Lord Vandover could have seen in her to prompt an offer.

"It...it all seems almost unreal, doesn't it?" she asked, as her mother moved to open the door. "Everything happened so quickly." Since her arrival in London in mid-September, her life had become one exciting whirl.

"'Twas the most romantic thing I ever saw," responded Mrs. Paxton with enthusiasm. "Who would have guessed you would take so well? And Vandover—so gallant, so handsome! A marquess—heir to the Duke of Wickburn!" She sighed happily, tipping her head to one side. "And he must have been thoroughly enchanted with you to make you an offer only a month into the Little Season. Such a coup for you—for us all!"

Blanche's face took on a pinched look, but Holly smiled dreamily into the mirror, remembering.

Of course she had accepted him. Not only did his title, wealth and looks place him head and shoulders above his rivals, as Maman had repeatedly pointed out, but he seemed to have a depth that went far beyond the shallow flirtation of her other suitors. His compliments, though few and never flowery, always sounded sincere. And, even more important, he seemed kind. But so serious. Holly had sensed a need in him, a hunger for happiness, for simple gaiety, that she immediately longed to fill.

She had fallen head over ears in love before she knew where she was.

Swept up in the wonder of her first romance, Holly had not recalled until just recently her brother's parting words. Wouldn't Noel be amazed when he discovered she had done just what he had jokingly advised—and through no real effort of her own. She chuckled, finally turning away from the glass.

"*Allons,* my love, come!" Her mother urged her through the door. "The others will be waiting by now. Blanche, *chérie,* you have my fan?"

Once she was out of the now-familiar chamber she had occupied during her two weeks at Wickburn, Holly's flash of humour unexpectedly gave way to near panic. There was no turning back now, she suddenly realized. Glitter and romance were all well and good, but marriage was for a lifetime—a lifetime to be spent with a man she barely knew.

Since asking for her hand two months ago, the marquess and Holly had enjoyed exactly three private conversations, all of them brief. She knew that he was used to having his own way—his insistence on a speedy wedding told her that much. What else might he insist upon? She tightened her grip on her mother's arm as they descended the grand staircase.

Mrs. Paxton merely patted her hand comfortingly. She had given her daughter reams of advice, both practical and cautionary, and pieces of it spun through Holly's head now.

"For all that he is plainly a passionate man, you must not be hurt if your marquess conceals his feelings. The English are not so open about their feelings as we French," she had said once. And then, only last night, "Pray have no fear of your wedding bed, my love. A little pain—tut!—what is that? 'Tis over in a flash, and many women feel none at all, only pleasure...."

Oddly, it was the Christmas decorations that helped to restore Holly's equilibrium. The drapings of greenery and the red velvet bows reminded Holly of Christmases past at her home in Derbyshire. Somehow, the familiar sharp scent of fir and the gleam of holly berries made the imposing Great Hall seem less intimidating.

At the same time, they reminded Holly again of how much she missed Noel, especially today, on Christmas Eve—their joint birthday. His absence lent the only melancholy note to what surely had to be the happiest day of her life. What *was* he doing all this time in France? So far he had sent no word.

Suddenly she was at the bottom of the grand staircase and all thoughts fled in the bustle around her. The dowager duchess, Lord Vandover's grandmother, was there, along with the Duchess of Wickburn, his stepmother. The duchess was strikingly lovely in pale green satin trimmed with white fur, her flame red hair piled elegantly beneath a matching bonnet that was the height of fashion. The marquess's sister, Lady Anne, stood close by, cheerful and pretty in a rose gown which matched Blanche's.

"Well, my dear, your day has arrived!" The dowager duchess, dressed in lilac velvet and looking remarkably lively for her eighty-odd years, came forward at once to clasp her hands. "Dare I hope you are as happy as I about it?"

Holly warmed instantly to the elderly woman's infectious cheerfulness. "Happier, I should hope, your grace," she responded, though somewhat breathlessly.

The dowager perceived it at once. "A bit nervous, are ye?" A touch of Irish lilt was noticeable in her voice. "That's to be expected, I suppose. You needn't be, though. Hunt will do well by you. If he don't, he'll answer to me!" She nodded vigorously, her blue eyes twinkling.

"Have the gentlemen gone on to the church already?" asked Holly's mother.

"Nearly ten minutes ago," replied the duchess, from behind the dowager. "We should hurry, Miss Paxton." Holly had a fleeting impression that the duchess's smile did not quite reach her eyes.

Then she was being bundled out the door and into the carriage waiting to convey the ladies to the ceremony. Wedged between the dowager and her mother, who chattered across her like magpies, Holly felt herself again swept up into the moment.

At the door of the church she felt her panic momentarily resurface. A throng of the local people waited without, ready to cheer and offer congratulations the moment the newlyweds emerged. Their presence underscored the fact that one day she would be duchess on these lands, with important responsibilities to these people. It seemed an awesome prospect.

Then, seemingly between one breath and the next, she was inside the church, with her mother and the dowager putting finishing touches to the set of her tiara and the fall of her lace. Music was struck up and the portly, jovial Duke of Wickburn himself stepped forward to escort her the length of the aisle to where the marquess awaited her. For just the merest moment, Holly wished that Noel could have been here to give her away, but then her eyes met those of her bridegroom and all her misgivings fled.

The marquess looked handsomer than she had ever seen him, attired in deep blue satin, the gold embroidery of his waistcoat picking up the matching highlights in his brown hair. At the sight of her, his clear blue eyes warmed and his firm lips curved in a slight smile.

Ashton Huntcliff Maitland, Marquess of Vandover, or "Hunt" to his friends, watched Holly's progress with pride. Amazing that he had found such a woman so soon after making the decision to wed. What a wife she would make him!

With her raven hair, ivory complexion and wide green eyes sparkling with laughter, Holly had offered a welcome contrast to his own sombre, world-weary outlook. Years of diplomatic missions, mostly abroad, trying to forge his own career while covering for his father's frequent blunders, had left him cynical almost to the point of bitterness. Holly's easy, open gaiety had drawn him like a moth to a flame.

Nor did she have any of the airs and affectations one would expect in one so lovely. Instead, she seemed totally unaware of her own charms, a vivid contrast to his step-mother, who demanded that everyone within her radius pay homage to her beauty. Watching Holly walking toward him, so elegant in her bridal finery, Hunt felt a surge of longing. Schooling her in love would be sheer delight—a delight that would begin tonight.

Finally completing the long, slow walk up the chapel aisle, Holly took her place at her bridegroom's side. As she repeated the vows, his eyes frequently sought hers and she felt a delicious warmth fill her at the promise in their expression. Their kiss at the conclusion was all too brief; she would have liked to explore further the interesting sensations that occurred at the touch of his lips on hers.

Holly floated on air during the return trip down the aisle on her new husband's arm. The wintry daylight that greeted them, as much as the cheers of the common folk, buoyed her spirits further—she had always loved winter. Glancing up at the sky, she wondered whether it might snow, to complete the perfection of this Christmas for her. But then, she recalled, that would cause travelling difficulties for the hundred or more guests who had come for the wedding. Snow in January would do just as well, she supposed.

"You make as beautiful a bride as I thought you would, Lady Vandover," the marquess whispered into her ear as he handed her into the decorated carriage that was to bear them back to Wickburn.

Holly blinked. *Lady Vandover*. The title sounded so strange, so new. She smiled. "And you make a very handsome bridegroom, my lord," she responded warmly, meaning every word. Surely, this was her happiest birthday ever.

As though divining her thoughts, her new husband drew her close against him in the private carriage as it began to move. "My Christmas bride. I'm glad I insisted upon a Christmas wedding instead of waiting until next summer, as the duchess wished us to do. Are you?"

Holly nodded happily. "'Twill make this special day even more so. Nor need I fear you will forget our anniversary, my lord," she teased.

"Nor your birthday, either." His answering chuckle delighted her, for Lord Vandover's apparent lack of humour had been her one reservation when she accepted him.

"But come," he continued. "Now we are married you must call me Hunt, as my friends do." He gazed down at her. "And what do your friends call you? Holly Berry perhaps?" She rolled her eyes at him in response. "Perhaps not. But I rather like it, I think. Come, Holly Berry—give your new husband a kiss."

She tipped her face up to him, smilingly surrendering her lips. He had kissed her only twice before the wedding, chaste kisses much like the brief brush of lips in the church. This was quite different.

Putting one arm about her shoulders, he pulled her to him gently. With his other hand he traced the curve of her face. His lips teased hers and she revelled in the masculine, spicy scent of him, the strength of him. As he deepened the kiss, the sensation she had briefly felt at the end of the ceremony rekindled and she responded eagerly. She felt his hands stroking her back and the nape of her neck, and the first real surge of desire she had ever experienced awoke within her.

Chuckling again, he put her gently away. "We will be at Wickburn in a moment, and I would not have our guests think me so impatient that I ravished my new bride on the drive from the church!"

The glitter in his eyes told her clearly that he very much wished to do just that. Absurdly, Holly felt herself blushing.

"Now your lips look like holly berries in truth." Then he became serious again. "Tonight cannot come too soon for my taste!"

She remained silent, suddenly recalling in detail what her mother had told her yesterday about the marriage bed. Would she be one of those fortunate women who felt little pain? Surely so. She could not imagine Lord Vandover—Hunt—hurting her.

Their carriage came to a stop before the ducal mansion and a footman lowered the steps. Nervously tucking a stray hair back into place beneath her veil, Holly emerged to another burst of cheering, this time from the extensive staff at Wickburn. More people who would one day be dependent upon her, she realized nervously, as she smiled brightly to the assemblage.

The dowager had promised to school her thoroughly in her duties, she reminded herself. With Hunt's stepmother and grandmother both here, surely little would be expected of her as yet. For today, at least, she would not worry about the future.

Guests from Yorkshire and the surrounding counties had been invited to the wedding breakfast, and nearly all were in attendance despite tomorrow being Christmas. The marriage of a duke's heir was no small occasion. Many would stay through the holiday season as well, Holly knew, recalling the flurry of preparation over the past few days. Tomorrow would be a happy Christmas, indeed.

Blushing again, she recalled that by tomorrow morning she would be indoctrinated into the mysteries of married life. But then, glancing up at Hunt's strong profile, she felt secure, even eager. It would be all right.

Though she had met many of the guests at her betrothal ball a fortnight since, Holly despaired of ever remembering the names and faces presented to her during the interminable reception. At length, though, the guests had filed past and the new couple were allowed to leave their posts by the door.

"Now for the next bit of pomp," murmured Hunt into Holly's ear. She smiled in relief at this evidence that he disliked the overwhelming formality as much as she did.

There were toasts and speeches by all and sundry to the health and future of the new marchioness, and then the orchestra began to play. Hunt led Holly out to begin the dancing.

"Only a few more hours, my sweet, then it will just be us," he whispered.

As they danced the minuet with their eyes locked, Hunt's gaze spoke volumes about the pleasures in store. Holly drank it in, her vague nervousness dissipated by champagne.

The rest of the afternoon and evening passed in an ecstatic blur. The only thing that marred the otherwise perfect day was Noel's absence and her nagging worries about him that could not quite be stilled. Had Uncle Henri found him a post where he could uncover useful information for the British? Had he found a way of communicating it? She longed to know.

Finding herself alone for a brief, breathless minute early in the evening, Holly was accosted by her new mother-in-law, Camilla, the Duchess of Wickburn.

"My dear, you are holding up wonderfully, I must say. Most girls would have wilted by now under the whirl you have been subjected to all day. How excessively strong you must be!" The duchess's lovely brown eyes were guileless, so Holly decided to interpret her words as a compliment.

"Yes, my mother often remarks on my energy, your grace."

"Ah, your dear mother! I trust she has given you some idea of what you may expect tonight? But then, I am forgetting—she is French. No doubt you have received a most *thorough* education in matters of that sort."

Holly regarded her doubtfully, trying hard to construe her meaning as other than an insult. "My mother spoke to me, yes," she replied carefully.

"Good, good!" The duchess showed her teeth in a breathtaking smile, though her eyes glittered with curiosity. "Then I need not add my own advice, I am sure. I vow, I was terrified on my own wedding night!" She lowered her eyes modestly. "My mama was English, you understand, and not so forward about such things."

Holly frowned slightly. "There is nothing forward about my mother, I assure you, your grace." Still, she strove to keep her tone polite. She would be spending a large part of her life in this woman's company, after all.

"Oh, no, of course not, dear," said the duchess quickly. "I merely meant that there are certain...differences between the English and the French. No offence was meant to your mother. Ah, there is dear Lady Mountheath! I have been trying to catch her for a word all afternoon. If you will excuse me, dear." She flitted away.

Differences? Did the duchess consider her marriage to Hunt to be unequal in some way? Unconsciously, Holly straightened her shoulders. Her family was as good as theirs. Papa had been a son of the Earl of Ellsdon, and Grand-père was a French comte, even if he *had* lost his lands in the Terror. And the Paxtons were a far older family than the Maitlands, dating back to the Norman invasion.

A touch on her arm recalled her to her surroundings. "Most of the guests have gone, you know. The ones that are left plan to stay the night. What do you say to slipping away?" Hunt's voice was low, but it thrummed with an emotion that struck an answering chord in Holly's midsection. At once, all thoughts of the duchess fled.

"I thought you'd never ask, my lord," she replied breathlessly, her heart hammering in her breast. Placing a hand on his sleeve, she accompanied her new husband from the ballroom, through the Great Hall and up the grand staircase.

CHAPTER TWO

"OH, HUNT, how lovely!" exclaimed Holly when he threw open the door to what would now be her suite. He'd had it redecorated for her, she knew, and this was the first time he had allowed her to see it. The sitting-room was done in vibrant floral tones, giving the impression of a garden. The wall hangings, upholstery and curtains were all new. Behind it was the bedchamber, more softly decorated in lilac and white. All Holly's favourite colours, in fact. How had he known?

"I'm glad it pleases you," said Hunt gravely, gazing down at her. "There is a dressing-room through that door—" he pointed "— and my own chambers just beyond. I'll show them to you . . . in the morning." He closed the door quietly and turning towards her, he lowered his lips to hers.

This kiss was even more thorough than the one in the carriage, and Holly felt she was drowning and coming alive all at the same time. Hunt began to unpin the lace veil from her hair.

"Should . . . should I ring for my maid?" she asked reluctantly.

"Not tonight, I think." His blue eyes were smoky now. "I will do her office instead."

He turned her around, removing her veil and undoing the tiny hooks down her back with deft fingers. His touch sent a shiver of anticipation through her. With firm hands on her shoulders, he pivoted her to face him again for another lingering kiss.

"You're not afraid. That's good."

Holly could not help recalling the duchess's words, but now, with Hunt so close, they had no power over her. She was nervous perhaps, and a little excited, but not afraid. "I want to make you happy, Hunt," she murmured against his throat as he held her. The deep chuckle she loved rumbled for an instant beneath her lips.

"You will, my sweet. I'll show you how." As carefully as her maid could have done, he removed the costly wedding dress and laid it aside. "And now your hair. I've wanted to run my hands through it since the first night I saw you." He unpinned the ebony mass one lock at a time, kissing her after each one, until she longed for him to finish and go on to whatever the next stage might be.

Finally, her hair was down and he stepped back. Holly felt oddly vulnerable clad in only her sheer chemise and the black mantle of her hair, but seeing the glow in Hunt's eyes, she relaxed.

He smiled. "Lovely. Even more so than I'd imagined. And now—" He drew her down with him to the bed.

Her mother had been right—there was nothing at all to be afraid of. Hunt was as gentle as he was thorough, slowly guiding her to a state of wondering arousal. At first Holly's inexperience hampered her response, but soon eagerness swamped hesitancy and she urged him on. The prick of pain she felt when he first entered her was quickly forgotten as other, pleasurable sensations took its place.

"Did I succeed?" she asked, as they lay cuddled together afterwards.

He rolled onto his side to regard her in surprise. "Succeed?"

"In making you happy."

His slow smile answered her. "Happier than I can ever remember being, my Holly Berry."

"Then you must be a good teacher," she said playfully. Now that the dreaded—and longed-for—first time was behind her, she felt liberated from the last vestiges of anxiety. "But surely I will need further lessons?"

Hunt's smile became a grin. "You are an apt pupil, my dear. We will run over the basics once more, I think, then move on to more advanced studies." He pulled her to him again and she responded eagerly.

As she finally drifted to sleep hours later, Holly felt as if a whole new world had opened up to her. The most amazing discovery of all was that she could bring Hunt such pleasure. It made her feel that theirs could not be such an unequal marriage, after all.

She was now truly Hunt's wife, she thought dreamily, his lady in every sense of the word. The years ahead glittered with promise. She would learn even more ways of pleasing him, both within the bedchamber and without. She would teach him to laugh, to enjoy life. And they would spend long hours talking, discovering everything about each other— becoming friends. Enveloped in happiness, she slept.

At the touch of Hunt's lips on hers, Holly awakened from a delicious dream to find the morning already well advanced. They had neglected to draw the bed curtains, and the morning light streamed in across them, picking out the golden highlights in her husband's hair as he gazed down at her. Holly's heart turned over. He looked so handsome, so loving.

"Good morning, sleepyhead," he said, a slight smile tugging at the corner of his mouth. "My, but you wake prettily." His eyes roved over her possessively.

Suddenly realizing that she had nothing on, not even a sheet, Holly blushed and his smile broadened.

"Such maidenly modesty! You needn't be embarrassed before me, my little Holly Berry—ever." He bent his head to hers and Holly quickly forgot her uncharacteristic shyness in a renewal of last night's pleasures.

A discreet tapping at the door roused them from a nap sometime later. The angle of the sun showed it to be past noon.

"My lord, my lady?" came the voice of Mabel, the smart young maid who had been assigned to Holly. "The duchess wishes to know if you will be down for Christmas dinner."

"By Jove! I'd dashed near forgot this was Christmas Day," whispered the marquess. Then, raising his voice, he called, "Give me five minutes, then you may come in to help your mistress dress." He gave Holly another kiss, but quickly. "They must have gone to service this morning without us. Grandmama's doing, I doubt not. I'm glad she managed to overrule Father and Camilla on it—I wouldn't have relished being wakened at sunrise!"

He never called the duchess "mother," Holly had noticed.

After one last embrace, he disappeared through the dressing-room door. Burning with embarrassment at what the maid would think, Holly called out for her to enter.

Though she smiled rather a lot as she fastened her new mistress into a cream wool morning gown, Mabel said nothing, for which Holly was profoundly grateful. She wondered how on earth she was going to face a houseful of people. They all must know why she and Hunt had missed the early morning church service. Just as she reached the door, however, the maid put her mind at rest on that point.

"Oh, I almost forgot, m' lady! Her grace, the dowager, wishes the family to attend evening service, as so many of the guests slept in this morning. Not surprising after the number of bottles they went through last night, if you ask me." She tittered at her own boldness.

Holly breathed a sigh of relief just as Hunt emerged from his chamber, conservatively dressed in dark blue and cream. He offered Holly his arm and together they went downstairs.

Christmas Day was one of the liveliest Holly could remember, mainly owing to the presence of Lady Anne's three children, as well as a few other youngsters who had come with their parents. They entered into the old traditions with such enthusiasm that even the adults got involved, exclaiming over gifts the children had made, playing blind man's bluff and putting on their own mumming play complete with Old Father Christmas, portrayed by the Duke of Wickburn himself.

The Christmas dinner served late that afternoon was the most extensive feast Holly had ever seen or imagined, dwarfing even the lavish buffets that had been spread to celebrate her wedding yesterday. Geese, capons and pheasants jostled for space on the groaning tables with jellies, tarts and trifles. Long before the splendidly blazing plum pudding was carried triumphantly from the kitchens, Holly was stuffed to capacity.

Across the table, Hunt sent her a wink and a slow, seductive smile that whetted her appetite even more than the fabulous food had. Her pulse quickened as she suddenly longed for Christmas Day, the happiest she'd ever spent, to draw to its close.

"WHEN I WAS a child, Boxing Day was always my favourite part of the whole Christmas season," Lady Anne confided to Holly as they paused just inside the barn where the traditional Feast of St. Stephen was being held. "In fact, I believe it is still."

Holly could understand why. On her own father's small estate, this day had been observed only perfunctorily, with gifts carried by servants to the poorer tenants. But she had already discovered that the Duke of Wickburn never did anything shabbily.

All the Wickburn tenants and villagers were gathered, along with the wedding guests, for a dance and celebration on the biggest of the tenant farms. Mr. Miller, the resident farmer, greeted people, noble or humble, as they entered, as graciously as though he were welcoming them to a fine ballroom furnished with gilt chairs, instead of a barn, decorated only with greenery and with bales of hay for seats.

The duke himself was plainly in his element, handing out cheeses, smoked sides of ham and brandied cakes to all and sundry, and directing the placement of the beer barrels himself. Hunt, by his side, seemed to be enjoying himself, as well, as did Lord Reginald, Hunt's half brother, and the Dowager Duchess Aileen. Class distinctions were apparently laid aside for this day—at least by most. The duchess stood off to one side, deep in conversation with Lady Mountheath and a few other high sticklers, apparently trying to ignore the peasantry.

When the gifts were all distributed, the band struck up a country tune and Wickburn led Mrs. Miller out for the first dance. With a wink at Holly, Hunt partnered old Mrs. Crockett, the butcher's wife, while Holly and Lady Anne seated themselves on bales of hay beside Anne's two youngest children.

"I cannot get over the change in Hunt since he met you!" Lady Anne exclaimed. "Why, in years past, 'twas all we could do to convince him to attend the St. Stephen's dance, much less join in the revelry. Only when Grandmama forbade him to work on estate or Foreign Office business would he come." She smiled warmly at Holly. "Thank you."

"He has always been so serious, then?" Holly had been drawn to Lady Anne from the first and hoped now to discover a bit more about Hunt, who was in many ways still a stranger to her.

"Oh, as a child he enjoyed these parties as much as I did, I believe. But with each passing year he has seemed to take more and more responsibility on himself, wrapping himself in duty, honour and protocol, until there was no room left for enjoyment—except on the hunting field, of course."

"Of course." Holly already knew of Hunt's fondness for fox-hunting. It was the reason she'd seen so little of him between their betrothal and marriage.

"But there he need not open himself up to people. I am so happy to see him regaining his ability to trust."

"To trust?" asked Holly curiously. "But why—"

At that moment, however, Anne's eldest son, William, ran full tilt into one of the beer kegs, knocking it over. His mother rose hastily to intercede in the ensuing argument between William and young Jeb Miller, another sturdy lad of seven, over whose fault it had been.

Before she returned, Holly was claimed for a dance by one of the local farmers. When she questioned Lady Anne later about her comment, Hunt's sister merely said vaguely that a combination of events in recent years had conspired to make Hunt close himself off from even his family.

"But now it is plain he has got over that phase, and is back to being the big brother I love and remember. What a marvellous Christmas present you've given me, Holly!"

It was plain that Lady Anne had no further wish to pursue the subject of Hunt's earlier problems, so Holly let the matter drop. Hunt himself came to claim her for a reel just forming, and in the revelry she found it easy to forget what was plainly in the past.

DURING THE DAYS that followed, Holly discovered that even though they were married, her only private moments with her husband were in her bedchamber at night. At least before the wedding, they'd had opportunities to talk, or to wander the estate, as they'd done during the mistletoe hunt the week before Christmas. But now her days were filled with games and excursions, singing and feasting, while the marquess and most of the gentlemen took advantage of the continued fine weather by hunting.

Each night there was a dance, fully as grand as any ball Holly had attended in London. It was usually long after midnight before she and Hunt could graciously retire, though once or twice the dowager nudged them up the back staircase earlier and made their excuses for them. In contrast, however, Holly sometimes received the impression that the Duchess of Wickburn disliked the very notion that she and Hunt spent their nights together, strange as that seemed.

The dowager, for her part, made no secret of the fact that she could scarcely wait to hold a great-grandchild in her arms. Owing to her machinations, Holly found herself beneath the kissing bough with amazing regularity. If anything, Hunt seemed more embarrassed than she by the frequent necessity to kiss before an audience. Holly's mother had been quite correct, it seemed, about English gentlemen's unwillingness to display their feelings, at least in public.

One evening, however, as the orchestra tuned their instruments for the nightly dancing, Hunt deliberately led her beneath the mistletoe and paused to kiss her lingeringly.

"Perhaps we should keep one of these delightful things up year-round," he suggested, surprising her further. Indeed, it seemed that her liveliness was helping Hunt to unbend somewhat, just as Lady Anne had said.

NEW YEAR'S EVE saw festivities nearly as magnificent as those of her wedding day a week earlier. The local gentry had been invited to partake in the revelry, and at intervals throughout the evening, groups of the common folk came wassailing to the door, singing their letting-in songs and bearing huge wooden bowls which were cheerfully filled with lamb's wool punch by the duke.

He would merrily call out, "There's nothing like a well-filled bowl/ To make the yuletide carols troll," or some other spur-of-the-moment rhyme, and everyone would laugh politely, as they always did at Wickburn's little sallies.

The other guests offered coins, which the wassailers graciously accepted before moving on to other, lesser estates. However, as nearly everyone in the county was here, Holly doubted whether they would receive much elsewhere.

"Ah, sister! This time 'tis I who have caught you beneath the mistletoe!" It was Lord Reginald, Hunt's half brother, and the apple of the duchess's eye. "Come, give me my due!" Reaching up, he plucked a berry from the mistletoe dangling at the centre of the raft of greenery above them and smilingly approached her.

Holly returned the brotherly kiss willingly. She liked Reginald, though she found him as impossible to take seriously as the duke, with his tendency to dramatics and his wildly coloured evening wear. Tonight he was clad in a red coat, red-and-white striped waistcoat, white breeches and bright red pumps. He looked like a giant stick of peppermint candy, she thought, stifling a giggle. It was a shame his hair was orangish rather than the flame red his mother possessed. That would have completed the effect.

"My, you look festive tonight," she managed to say with a tolerably straight face after they had exchanged their peck.

"I thought it appropriate for New Year's Eve. I have convinced Father to let me be tonight's first footer, as well. Just west of here, red hair is considered the luckiest colour, you know."

Holly smiled—indeed, it was hard to do otherwise around Reginald. "In that case, I will consider your kiss a wonderful omen for the year ahead."

Reginald grinned. "I hope so. I can scarcely wait to have another niece or nevvy to spoil, as I've told Hunt repeatedly." He waggled his brows and winked. Then, bowing deeply, he sauntered off to find a partner for the next set.

Just then, she caught sight of the duchess dotingly following Lord Reginald's progress and her smile faded. Could that be why her mother-in-law seemed less than enchanted with the idea of Hunt's producing an heir? At this moment, Reginald was next in the succession, but any son Holly bore would preempt him. At least, Reginald himself did not seem put out by that prospect, thank heaven.

Holly forced a smile back to her lips and turned away to find Hunt. Together they would bring the duchess round in time, she thought optimistically. Noel had always said she had a knack for setting people at ease.

ONLY ONCE during the Christmas festivities did Holly and the marquess manage to slip away together during daylight hours. The morning after New Year's Day, Hunt whisked her out of the house just after breakfast to show her his kennels.

"This is one of the finest packs of foxhounds in all England, if I do say so myself," he informed her proudly. She leaned over the rail to look at the enthusiastic residents of the large straw-floored enclosure. Holly's father had kept his dogs kennelled at one end of the barn, but Hunt had an entire building devoted to them.

"They're wonderful," she agreed. "Have you directed their breeding yourself?"

He glanced at her in surprise. "Why yes, I have. You speak as if you know something about it."

She smiled, her eyes still on the hound she was patting as it stood on its hind legs against the gate. "Father kept a pack, though now we only have old Arrow. Father sold the rest to Mr. Danvers after he fell ill, but Arrow was too old for the hunt."

"Your father was a sportsman, then?"

Holly nodded, realizing anew how little they really knew about each other. "He was nigh as enthusiastic about it as you are," she said with a twinkle. "'Twas why he originally purchased in Derbyshire, I believe."

"And your brother? Does he not hunt?"

Holly tried to ignore the pang she always felt when she thought of Noel, far away and possibly in danger—a danger she was not allowed to share. "Oh, yes, he loves it. Doubtless he will start his own pack when he...returns home. He may even buy back some of the offspring of Father's hounds, as he had a hand in their breeding."

They continued to converse on that and other topics for another quarter hour before some of the other gentlemen came looking for her husband to form yet another hunting party while the weather held so fine.

Holly looked forward to more such precious moments once the guests were gone.

CHAPTER THREE

ON THE SEVENTH of January, the visitors finally began to depart. The decorations had been removed the day before, after gifts were exchanged and the Twelfth Cake eaten. The Christmas season was officially over.

Though Holly had expected to feel mainly relief at the end of the holidays, she was surprised to feel a pang of regret. For the rest of her life, she knew she would associate the Twelve Days of Christmas with her initiation into womanhood, with love, with happiness—and with Hunt. Still, life would surely assume a more normal flow now, allowing her and Hunt the time—finally—to really get to know each other.

"I hope the news from Russia continues good, sir," said Hunt in parting to Lord Matherly, one of the last to leave. "When I join you in London this spring, we may be ready to forge a new treaty, after all."

Holly stood beside her husband, listening intently, as she always did when anything to do with the war or politics was discussed. It happened all too infrequently in her hearing, she found. But Lord Matherly's next words, while indisputably related to the war, filled her with dismay rather than satisfaction.

"Spring!" he said in surprise. "Did Wickburn not tell you? Castlereagh requires all of us in Town almost immediately to put plans together for a meeting with the Prussians and Austrians in April."

"Immediately? But—"

"I know you'd hoped for a bit of a honeymoon, m' boy." Lord Matherly smiled at Holly, his expression sympathetic. "But these things can't be helped. A man in your position—and your father's, too, of course—" he glanced hastily over to where Wickburn and the duchess were speaking with Lady Matherly "—has to expect these demands as we forge new alliances. War waits for no man, I'm afraid."

"Well I know it," replied Hunt. Holly thought he sounded bitter.

Lord Matherly went to join his wife, and Hunt turned to her. "I'd hoped nothing like this would arise before spring," he said ruefully. "It was one reason I wanted us to marry now, rather than wait, for there seemed a greater possibility of interruption or delay later."

"Can I not come to Town with you?" she asked eagerly. "I should like to meet all of the diplomats."

Hunt sadly shook his head, reminding her forcibly of Noel. "Not this time. Wickburn House has only a skeleton staff right now, and I've had no chance as yet to look about for a place of our own. I shall be back in time to escort you down for the Season, though, I promise. You'll be quite a hit with the old men of the Foreign Office, unless I miss my guess." He managed a strained smile.

Touched by his obvious reluctance to leave her, Holly forced herself to smile back. "What precisely is it that you do in the Foreign Office, Hunt? You have never told me."

His smile twisted slightly, but he answered readily enough. "Despite what Matherly says, I'm not so indispensable, really. Just one of numerous deputy foreign ministers. For the most part, I oversee aspects of wartime communications and occasionally intelligence."

"Intelligence?" Holly echoed. "Do you mean spies? How very exciting!" Could Hunt possibly know something of Noel? She wished she dared ask, but of course she had given Noel her word.

But Hunt only laughed. "Not nearly so much as you make it sound, I assure you. By far the preponderance of my time is spent moving mounds of dull papers from one stack to another. But you needn't worry your lovely head over it, my dear. When you do come to London in the spring, I shall introduce you to far more amusing diversions."

Though she was a bit nettled by his condescension, Holly let the matter drop, for the Matherlys were leaving and she was called upon to play her part as under-hostess.

Holly and Hunt tried hard to spend as much time together as possible during the two days before he and his father left for London, but he was frequently busy with last-minute estate business—business he had thought to have months rather than days to conduct.

"Brother, I always knew the government was heartless, but this goes beyond anything they've done yet," said Lord Reginald to Hunt the morning of his departure, as they descended the stairs together. "Cannot this business wait till a more propitious time? I don't like to see you abandoning your new bride this way, and neither does Grandmama. She told me so last night."

"She has told me so as well, at length." Hunt sighed. "And she is right, of course, though it was she who was so insistent I marry this year. But what can I do? Duty calls."

"I believe you think too much of your vaunted duty," remarked Reginald.

Hunt scowled at his half brother. "As you think too little of it?"

Reginald spread his hands wide. "I do try, you know. Occasionally Grandmama even trusts me to construct a menu or attempt some other task that won't suffer too much from my absence of mind. But generally she loses patience with my feeble efforts and sends me back to my canvases." He shrugged, with a self-deprecating grin.

Reluctantly, Hunt grinned back. After all, it wasn't Reg's fault he had to go to Town. Besides, he had never been able to hold out against his brother's clownish charm, not even when, as a rapscallion of five, Reg had dumped a box of bath salts on his fifteen-year-old brother's head, severely deflating Hunt's adolescent self-importance. Looking back at his brother, he said, "You and Grandmama take care of Holly while I'm gone, all right?"

Reginald nodded. "Of course. But here they are now."

Holly and the dowager came around the corner at the foot of the stairs just as Hunt and Lord Reginald reached the bottom. "I should have known I'd find you together," Hunt said, reaching out with one hand to gently stroke his wife's rose petal cheek. "Has Grandmama put you to work already?"

He deliberately kept his tone light, for he knew this parting was as difficult for Holly as for himself. Their lovemaking last night, and again early this morning, had been especially tender. She was proving even more apt a pupil than he had dared hope. Hunt ached for what he would miss while he was gone.

"There is quite a lot to be done, it appears, after the upheaval of the holidays," Holly said, smiling tremulously up at him. "Grandmama was showing me where the medicines for the charity baskets are kept."

"'Twill be a welcome change to have a willing—and *capable*—assistant," said the dowager briskly. Though she frowned ferociously at Reginald as she spoke, her eyes twinkled merrily. "Don't know that I'd have ever encouraged your dabbling, m' boy, had I known how incompatible art is with *real* work." The duke and duchess appeared at the head of the stairs just then, and the dowager converted whatever other remark she'd been about to make into a cough.

"Have you sent to have the carriage brought round yet?" called Wickburn as they descended.

Hunt nodded. "It should be at the door in a moment." He turned back to Holly.

"I can trust Grandmama to keep you busy in my absence, I suppose." He tried again to smile, but seeing her standing there so valiantly, he suddenly crushed her in an embrace, surprising himself as much as everyone around them. "I'll be back as soon as I possibly can," he whispered, then kissed her almost fiercely. She responded instantly, but he reluctantly let her go. There was no point in frustrating them both.

"You must do whatever is required in Town," she replied with commendable bravery, her chin high, though her green eyes shimmered with unshed tears. "I have plenty to learn here to keep me occupied for however long it takes."

The duke and duchess were beside them now, and Deeds, the butler, was announcing that the carriage was at the door. With a final swift kiss and a murmured endearment, Hunt accompanied his father outdoors, regretting, for the first time in his thirty years, the path his life had taken.

EVEN WITH HUNT, the duke and all the guests gone, Holly found that her time was nearly as occupied as it had been during the holidays. True to her word, the dowager launched her into an intensive course of study on the responsibilities facing a future Duchess of Wickburn.

"I passed eighty last year, my girl, so you'd best take advantage of my advice while you may," the dowager said more than once when she perceived Holly's attention slipping away from routine management tasks. "I won't be here forever, you know." Watching the vigorous old woman as she deftly arranged the contents of a food basket for one of the poorer tenants, Holly found that rather hard to believe.

Though her mind frequently strayed to Hunt and their brief time together, Holly absorbed fact upon fact from the dowager, learning both by listening and by doing.

"Much of the routine business was allowed to slide during the holidays," the dowager informed her as they inventoried the plate and silver. "We have some catching up to do."

Indeed they did, Holly found: medicines and necessities to deliver to the poorer families, inspections of the various servants' work. She was amazed at how intimately involved the dowager was in such tasks, tasks that her own mother, and Blanche, who in recent years had taken over the management of the household, always left to Mary, the housekeeper.

In addition, she learned many aspects of estate management, for as the duke and Hunt had been so frequently abroad on diplomatic missions over the years, the dowager had taken on those duties, as well. Holly was also required to learn the names of all the servants, from the haughty Norris, groom of the chambers, down to little Alice, the under-scullery maid. She rather doubted that the current duchess could name a single one of the lower servants, and she took pride in her growing ability to do so.

"Why does the duchess never accompany us to the village?" she asked at one point, when she had grown comfortable enough with the dowager to indulge her habitual curiosity. Holly had expected to miss Maman, as this was the first time in her life she had been separated from her, but she found Hunt's grandmother often filling her role as confidante.

"Camilla!" responded the dowager with a snort, her hands buried in the pungent dried herbs she was mixing for a restorative tea. "She can't be bothered with this humdrum stuff. She's far too busy primping and making calls to learn the *real* responsibilities required of a duchess. But there! You've made me say what I shouldn't, for she did bring happiness back into Wickburn's life after dear Marian's death. For that I suppose I must be grateful to her, though it's hard to forgive what she did to Hunt."

"To Hunt?" asked Holly curiously, wondering if this were what Lady Anne had referred to.

"For years he wouldn't accept her taking his mother's place," the dowager told her. "Not until he reached his teens and began to develop a fondness for Reggie. Then he did make an effort, but she'd have naught to do with him—fair pushed him away, and he little more than a child. It's a good thing I was here, or I'm not sure what he'd have done. But there! I'm rambling on again. Hold this cheesecloth for me while I sift the herbs into it."

Holly let the subject drop and went back to work. It was apparent that this constant activity, and the sound knowledge that she was needed, were what kept the dowager young. Holly wanted to believe that was the reason the duchess made no move to assist the dowager but was coming to see that the current Duchess of Wickburn was an idle, vain and rather silly woman who had little interest in what went on beyond her own little world.

While Holly could have forgiven her that, for her own mother and sister were not so very different in that respect, she doubted now that she'd ever fully forgive her for what she'd done to her stepson. He'd needed a mother so badly. Gradually, through snippets dropped by the dowager, a picture emerged of Hunt's teens and early adulthood, when he was alternately flattered and repulsed by Camilla and largely ignored by the duke—a picture that tugged at Holly's heart.

As January passed into February and winter gradually loosened its hold on the countryside, Holly also began to understand for the first time that far more was involved in being a successful woman than making a brilliant match or being admired by others. There was success in being useful, in gaining self-respect.

Still, there were times when she grew despondent, missing Maman and Noel, and especially her husband. How could she complete his transformation into a happy, outgoing man when he was more than a hundred miles away? When he and the duke finally returned to Wickburn on the first of March, she flew ecstatically out of the door to greet him.

"Welcome home, darling," she cried, flinging herself into his arms as he stepped from the travelling coach.

Not until he stiffened slightly in her embrace did she recall his reluctance to display affection in public. Through her conversations with the dowager, she had come to know her husband extremely well. Unfortunately, Hunt had not had the same advantage. Suddenly embarrassed, she started to pull back.

But he stopped her. "I vow, I've never had so warm a welcome before." His smile was slow, as though he was out of practice. "It makes leaving almost worthwhile. I missed you, my Holly Berry." With just one sheepish glance at the assembled family and servants looking on, he bent his head to kiss her.

"WE LEAVE FOR LONDON in two days' time," Hunt commented over breakfast a few days later. He had a huge stack of correspondence beside him, but was for the moment ignoring it to smile tenderly at her. "Would you care to stop for a day or two in Derbyshire to visit your mother?"

Holly had been basking in his undivided attention in the empty breakfast parlour, since Hunt had been unbelievably busy about the estate since his return, but at his question she gasped with delight. "Oh, may we? I must admit I have been just the tiniest bit homesick. And it would mean so much to Maman, I know."

Already she had begun to view her earlier life with the rosy tint of nostalgia for a simpler time. Forgotten were Blanche's slights, her mother's occasionally tiresome chatter. To relax in her old home for a few days, with Hunt by her side, sounded heavenly. And . . . perhaps there would be word from Noel.

"Of course we may. My presence will not be necessary in Town until late next week, and Father won't be there before Friday. At any rate, he and Camilla travel far more slowly than I prefer. This way we may set our own pace."

Accordingly, they set off early in the marquess's own carriage, a few hours ahead of the others. Hunt rode alongside the carriage much of the way and persuaded Holly to do likewise.

"I hate travelling with Camilla," he confided when they were out of earshot of the coachman. "She gets mortally offended if I choose to ride and insists on stopping every five miles or so. Of course, at the rate she makes poor John drive, that's still at least an hour between stops."

"Perhaps the motion of the coach makes her ill," suggested Holly. Though she now understood the reasons behind Hunt's unfilial attitude towards his stepmother, she still had hopes of eventually healing the breach between them. "You cannot blame her for that."

"I suppose not," he conceded. "But I needn't enjoy it, either!"

They kept a good pace, stopping only to change horses, and reached Tidebourne, Holly's old home, well before dusk. As they drew up before the front door, it opened and her mother appeared in the doorway. There was no sign of Blanche.

"Come in, my dear, my lord. How delightful a surprise is this! Why did you not send word ahead? No fear, though, we will manage."

"I knew you would put yourself out if you knew we were coming, Maman," said Holly, dismounting. "We will only be staying a day or two, and if we can but have a fire lit in my old room, we will go on splendidly." She concluded with a kiss on her mother's cheek.

"I sent Mary to attend to it as soon as I saw you arrive," Mrs. Paxton replied, effusively returning Holly's embrace.

They all went into the parlour, where Blanche was occupied in painting a small table with remarkably ugly brown flowers.

"Good evening my lady, my lord," she said formally as they entered. "How kind of you to drop by."

"Blanche!" exclaimed Holly with a laugh. "You needn't call me 'my lady.' I still have a name."

"I thank you for the liberty. I do hope you will find lamb chops to your liking for supper. Had we known you were coming, I doubt not Maman would have saved the ducks for your arrival rather than let Cook prepare them for dinner."

Holly saw Hunt's jaw tighten as it had once or twice before when the duchess made one of her tactless comments about Holly's nationality. On one of those occasions he had reprimanded his stepmother with a sharpness that startled Holly.

Even though, she thought guiltily, she might enjoy seeing him put Blanche in her place similarly, she knew it would make their visit less pleasant. "Lamb chops will be perfectly adequate, of course," she said quickly. Then, turning to her mother, "If you don't mind, I will go up to put off my cloak before tea."

Her room looked much as it ever had, a cheerful fire already crackling in the grate in testimony to Mary's efficiency. Mabel, her abigail from Wickburn, already awaited her there, a suitable gown laid out to replace Holly's habit.

Quickly, she helped her mistress to change, then sat her at the dressing-table to repair the disarray riding had caused to her hair. Holly glanced through a small pile of letters that had arrived in her absence while Mabel repinned it.

Most were congratulations on her recent marriage from the surrounding folk, but near the bottom she came upon a folded sheet addressed to her in a hand she well recognized, though the writer had made an effort to disguise it.

It was from Noel.

CHAPTER FOUR

"MY HAIR IS FINE, Mabel, thank you," said Holly as casually as she could manage, picking up a different letter and breaking the seal. "You may go."

The moment she was alone, she dropped the letter she was holding and tore open Noel's. So eager was she to know the contents that it took her a moment to realize that Noel had written it in their old childhood code—the code they had shared with no one else. It had been years since Holly had seen it, and though she herself had helped to devise it, for one panicked instant she feared that she had forgotten how it worked.

The memory came rushing back. It would read from bottom to top, of course, and from right to left. Every third word would be a nonsense word, and the others, their letters staggered by four so that *A* equalled *D* and *Y* equalled *B*, alternated French, Italian, German and English, in all of which she and Noel were fluent. Really, it was a rather clever code, she thought, particularly given that they were but fourteen years old when they invented it.

Carefully, she worked out the message. "Sorry this is so long reaching you," it read. "I am sending it by way of America. Took ship to France and am safe in Paris. Have clerk position, making useful connections. Essential you maintain secrecy. Reply only in code. Send to M. Broux, Dover. Shall advise of changes if possible. I pray everyone is well and your debut was successful."

Tears of relief trickled from the corners of her eyes as she read it through again to be sure. Noel was safe, or had been two months ago. Silently, she offered up a prayer of thanks.

"Ah, here you are! The tea is ready," Maman greeted her when she reentered the parlour a moment later.

Holly chattered cheerfully about their journey as she poured out, her relief over Noel's safety giving her added animation. Hunt was regarding her curiously, she noticed, but of course he could have no idea as to the reason for her added bounce. She smiled brilliantly at him as she handed him his cup, and he seemed to relax, rewarding her with the twinkle that appeared ever more frequently in his eyes of late.

After tea, Holly gave Hunt a tour of the rambling manor house. Fresh from the dowager's instruction, she could not help noticing certain things about Tidebourne that needed improvement. Small repairs were left undone, and at least one of the maids was shirking her cleaning duties, but she decided against antagonizing Blanche by mentioning them.

Indeed, Holly intended to thoroughly enjoy this brief hiatus, away from the responsibilities of Wickburn. When they reached London, she would have to learn a whole new set of rules and duties, this time under Camilla's tutelage. But for now, she could relax and spend some quiet time with her husband.

The next morning, Holly led Hunt down to the empty kennels, recalling his interest in foxhounds. "We have only old Arrow now, as I mentioned before, but you can see how Father designed the enclosure," she said, pointing to the half of the barn that housed it.

"Very efficient use of the space, I must say. This area was for whelping, I presume?"

Holly nodded eagerly. "Yes, and we had some fine pups born here. Why, Mr. Assheton-Smith himself once sent to inquire about purchasing a couple of them."

Hunt's eyebrows rose gratifyingly. "Quite a local legend, your father's pack, I perceive. Perhaps I shall check round to have a look at those you mentioned before. They were sold to a farmer hereabouts, you said?"

"Yes, Mr. Danvers, at Humblegate Farm. I must admit, I still miss Belltongue and Saddleback. They were rather pets of mine."

Leaving the kennel, Holly went on to show Hunt round some of her favourite childhood haunts. Before receiving Noel's letter she'd have been reluctant to visit those spots with anybody but her beloved brother. Now, knowing him to be safe, she was able to enjoy seeing them with her husband. He asked her occasional questions about the neighbourhood and she answered cheerfully, pleased to be sharing some of her background with him.

A day spent in such restful pursuits lent both of them added ardour in bed that night.

"Mmm. If that was my reward for bringing you to visit your home, we must make more such trips in the future," said Hunt afterwards.

"Taking me to London will entitle you to a reward, as well," Holly replied, snuggling close to him. "But I have enjoyed today tremendously, I must admit."

"Most of your memories of Derbyshire are happy ones, are they not?" Hunt's smile looked almost wistful.

Sensing that he was thinking of his own childhood, she nodded. "Yes, Noel and I were forever inventing games and romping about the countryside. Blanche tried to get us in trouble with Papa occasionally, especially when we played pranks on her, but that only added to the excitement—finding ways to cause mischief without being found out."

"I must keep a careful eye on you, I see. Else I may find spiders in my pockets someday."

Holly giggled. Not since Noel had left for France had she felt so lighthearted. "My lord!" she said with mock dignity. "Surely you cannot think the Marchioness of Vandover would stoop to such childish tricks? My mischief-making is far more sophisticated now, I assure you!''

He laughed with her and soon their humour gave way to passion. Lying wakeful by his side afterwards as he slept, Holly felt even happier than she had on her wedding day. She and her husband were becoming friends, as well as lovers—and Noel was safe.

''PERHAPS WE can go to visit that farmer you mentioned, the one who bought your father's pack,'' Hunt suggested as they rose from the breakfast table the next morning. ''What was his name?''

''Mr. Danvers,'' said Holly eagerly. It would be marvellous if Hunt were to buy some of them back. ''I can give you directions to Humblegate Farm—'tis not difficult at all to find, and no more than three miles from Tidebourne.''

''You don't wish to come along?'' He was plainly surprised.

In truth, Holly would have very much liked to accompany him, but had more pressing uses for the brief time he would be gone. ''I promised Maman that I would try to visit an old servant while I was here,'' she improvised. ''This would be a perfect opportunity.'' The moment he left, she hurried upstairs to answer Noel's letter.

She found it more difficult than she had expected, but not because of the code. How would Noel feel about the news of her marriage? He had told her to make a good match, of course, but she did not think he had really expected her to. Would he be hurt to hear she had married so quickly, not waiting for his return?

Finally, she composed her message, keeping the wording cool and precise, trying to convey her satisfaction at marrying Hunt, and Maman's, as well. At least Noel need not worry that she had wed someone unworthy of her. Protective as he had always been, she knew that would be the first thing he would suspect, just as she would, if Noel married—she could not imagine a woman who could deserve her brother. Smiling, she signed and sealed the letter, addressing it as Noel had instructed.

Did she have time to post it now? She would have to take it into the village herself, for she could not risk one of the servants gossiping about it. Hunt had been gone only half an hour—she should be back before he returned.

Holly felt a slight pang at keeping the matter from her husband, but she quickly subdued it. This matter had nothing to do with their marriage, and she had faithfully promised Noel to tell no one. Besides, it was rather exciting to have a secret. Pulling on her cloak, she slipped out of the house to walk the mile to the village.

While there, Holly bought a new bonnet and some ribbon so that she would have something to show for her errand, stopping at the post office last. No one was there but the postmistress, who was not the gossiping sort, so she was back outside in under a minute. She had not taken two steps, however, when she heard hooves behind her.

"Well met, my dear!" exclaimed Hunt, pulling to a halt and swinging down from the saddle. "Why did you not tell me you needed things from the village? I would have obtained them for you."

Holly strove to appear natural, though she could feel her cheeks burning guiltily. "I, ah, wanted to walk. 'Tis a lovely day, is it not?" Though he could have no reason to suspect her real mission, he frowned slightly at her flustered response. Desperately, she tried to think of something that might account for it.

"You...you are not angry that I came alone, are you, Hunt?" she asked on sudden inspiration. The duchess, she recalled, had been adamant that she not go about unaccompanied at Wickburn.

His brow cleared, to her relief. "Of course not. This is not London. Everyone knows you here. You need not act the marchioness if you would rather not."

Holly gave an exaggerated sigh. "Thank you—I would much rather not, actually. The townsfolk might think I was putting on airs."

He fell into step beside her, leading his horse. "I understand. But, believe it or not, you may find occasions in Town when it will be quite useful to put on airs."

"Indeed!" Holly grasped eagerly at the change of subject offered, seeing it as a chance to satisfy a portion of her insatiable curiosity, as well. "Pray tell me, what *can* I expect when we arrive in London, Hunt? You will introduce me to all of your associates at the Foreign Office, will you not?"

"Of course. But I fear you will find most of them as deadly dull as myself. Aging diplomats and bespectacled secretaries, for the most part, though a few of the foreign ambassadors are rather more interesting."

"If they are indeed as dull as yourself, I daresay I will find them a vastly amusing crowd," replied Holly, smiling up at him. "You do not give yourself enough credit."

"With your help I am improving, I think." He reached out and took her hand. "'Tis you who will be a credit to me, Holly. I believe you will bring some much-needed liveliness to those stuffy official functions."

DESPITE HUNT'S predictions, Holly did not find her first diplomatic gathering at all stuffy. There were issues of vital importance seething just below the surface, so many fascinating secrets to uncover, she was sure, if only she were to ask the right questions of the right people. But though she burned with curiosity and yearned to play some vital role in the affairs of the Foreign Office, she tried—at first—to limit herself to being agreeable.

She chatted with ambassadors and their wives, putting them at their ease by addressing many of them in their native tongues. Her fluent Italian, German and even French now stood her in good stead. Only the Russians baffled her, for she'd had no schooling in that language whatsoever. But even the Russians spoke English, and she soon had made many acquaintances.

"You are even more of a success than I predicted," Hunt murmured to her at one point, bringing her a glass of ratafia. "Quite the belle of the evening, in fact."

There was no dancing tonight, only conversation and a light buffet, but the rooms of the Foreign Office were decorated as lavishly as those of any private home. Only the exotic mixture of foreign accents and the undercurrent of political tension set this party apart from the lavish routs Holly had attended during her debut last fall.

She and Hunt were talking to one of the diplomats' wives when Lord Reginald came up to them with a young man at his side. He swept them an elaborate bow.

"Hunt, you know Teasdale, don't you?" he asked. Hunt nodded. "I wanted to introduce him to Holly. He's still fairly new to Town, and I'd noticed how good she is at making folks feel comfortable. Teasdale, m' sister-in-law, Lady Vandover."

The young man bowed over her hand. "Charmed, I'm sure." To her surprise, his accent was purely English.

"But surely you are no foreign ambassador, Mr. Teasdale," she said with a smile.

"Nay, merely a lowly clerk," he replied. He was nearly as tall as Hunt, but very thin, with a narrow clever-looking face and carefully combed pale hair. "Lord Reginald was kind enough to put in a good word for me with Wickburn."

"So you are a recent addition to the Foreign Office?"

He nodded. "And to London, as well. I arrived from Suffolk less than a month ago, in hopes of finding employment—youngest of four sons and all that. I was fortunate enough to encounter Reg at the Royal Academy a few days since."

"Yes, Teasdale and I were together at Eton," Reginald chimed in, enthusiastically waving his spy glass at the end of its ribbon. "We discovered there a common interest in art, but lost touch when I went on to Oxford. I'm delighted to have found him again."

"I fear I had only interest, while Lord Reginald has true talent," said Teasdale modestly, "but I, too, am most pleased to renew our acquaintance."

"Come, Mr. Teasdale," said Holly brightly before the conversation could turn to art, as it so often did around Reginald. "You must tell me about your new duties here. I vow, I find everything to do with the Foreign Office utterly fascinating."

"FOR THE FIRST TIME, I can honestly say I enjoyed a diplomatic affair," said Hunt after they returned to Wickburn House later that night. "And I have you to thank, Holly." They were alone in the sumptuous bedchamber he had refurnished for her during his earlier visit to Town.

Holly smiled up at him as she pulled off her gloves. "Perhaps you have simply learned to relax a bit. There is generally amusement to be found almost anywhere if one is but willing to look for it." She smoothed the gloves with her fingers before turning to lay them on her dressing-table.

"If only it were so easy." The wistfulness in his voice made her turn back quickly to search his face.

"It can be, Hunt. You...need not shoulder everyone's burdens, you know." He stared at her almost incredulously, and she hastened to explain. "Your grandmother and I had quite a lot of time for conversation while you were away. She told me how, for many years now, you have taken on responsibilities that should rightly be your father's, both on the estates and with the Foreign Office. She said you have closed yourself off from the diversions most gentlemen pursue."

"Except for hunting." His rueful smile made her heart expand with relief. She had half expected that he would either retreat into silence, as the dowager had said he used to do, or rebuke her for her impertinence. "Grandmama does not give herself enough credit, plainly. It is she who has kept Wickburn running during these past several years, with little or no help from Camilla, while father and I were off pursuing the phantom of peace across all of Europe."

"Surely since his defeat in Russia, Napoléon has lost most of his support. Peace cannot be so very far away now."

His smile was tender now. "So you heard more than compliments tonight, did you? But I fear he is already raising another army. The Russians and Prussians— But you cannot care about the politics of the situation, my dear. Come, turn round and I will unpin your hair."

Holly sighed, but turned obediently, her pulse already quickening. During the fortnight after their wedding, Hunt's unpinning of her hair had become a nightly ritual, one he had resumed upon his return. Always, it culminated with the two of them in bed, indulging in pleasures Holly was coming to enjoy more and more.

Slowly, lingeringly, he removed the last of the pins and turned her to face him. Lowering his mouth to hers, he slid his hands up her back to unfasten her gown. Political discussions could wait, Holly decided.

As THE SEASON APPROACHED, more members of the ton arrived in London, generating an overwhelming array of social activities. Almost from the moment she awoke, Holly's days were filled with breakfasts, levees, teas and soirées. There were trips to museums and the opera, shops and the theatre. To her disappointment, however, she saw little of Hunt after their first few days in Town.

Camilla arranged their social calendars. It was the one thing at which she excelled, and for which Hunt did not take responsibility. She generally strove to accommodate the maximum number of events, which often meant that the marquess was expected at one gathering while his wife attended another. In addition, there were developments at the

Foreign Office that required the frequent presence of Hunt and the duke.

On more than one occasion, Holly attempted to discover from him what was going on. Invariably, he brushed her questions aside, telling her that it was not her concern.

"If it concerns you it concerns me, Hunt," she said one evening. "How can I be a supportive wife to you if you will not tell me what worries you?"

"None of the other wives seem interested in prying into government affairs," he told her rather sharply. "And with good reason, for they are not nearly so interesting as you seem to believe. At any rate, this current matter is of a rather sensitive nature."

Holly seethed with frustration but said no more. She suspected that Hunt did not consider curiosity to be a particularly admirable trait. Still, she was determined to discover what she could, and decided to undertake a campaign of innocent-seeming questions at the next diplomatic function they attended.

Her father-in-law was especially unguarded in his answers, and she was able to determine that the current problem concerned an internal matter rather than international events. But just what that internal matter was she could not discover without making more pointed queries. At least Noel's mission—and safety—were not likely to be involved.

"Holly, my dear," said the duchess, coming up on Reginald's arm as they all prepared to leave. "I cannot get over what a success you are proving to be this Season. Positively everyone has something to say about you." Reginald nudged her slightly. "Something good, of course," she quickly qualified. "But then I have always heard that Frenchwomen are far better than we English at making friends, particularly with the gentlemen." She winked playfully.

"I assure you, your grace, that I consider myself more English than French. I've never even visited that country,"

Holly replied, thinking involuntarily of Noel, who was there even as she spoke.

"Indeed, Camilla," put in Hunt coldly, "I pray you will not say such things. You will have people thinking Holly is fast, when she is perfectly conformable."

Though she was not sure she considered that completely a compliment, Holly was glad of her husband's support. The duchess had still not entirely forgiven her, she thought, for threatening to cut Reginald out of the succession. Still, by and large she was more amiable than she had been at first, and Holly dared to hope that in time they might even become friends.

ACROSS THE DINNER TABLE the next evening, Hunt could not help noticing his wife's avid attention as the duke related, at her request, another tale of the exploits of the celebrated military-intelligence officer Colquhoun Grant.

"Why, he even managed to smuggle information out after the French captured him in Spain last year, from confinement. Then he escaped from his escort on the way to France and sent information to Wellington about Napoléon's plan to invade Russia." The duke chuckled.

"There are others, less well known, as well, are there not?" she asked eagerly. "Spies in France not connected with the military at all?"

The duke nodded. "By no means are all the French in sympathy with Boney. Some of those who've grown tired of him willingly give us news, either directly or through our own agents there. There are even some private British citizens who have gone to France solely for that purpose."

"Are there really? What sort of help have they been?" Her complete attention was on the duke, and he preened under it, rather to Hunt's amusement.

"Some have been more trouble than help," he said, "ending up as prisoners of war, bargaining tools for Napoléon. But some have sent us very valuable information indeed. Why there is one fellow, calls himself 'Puss in Boots'—''

Hunt cleared his throat warningly and his father hesitated, then smiled apologetically. "Perhaps I should limit my tales to years past, my dear. Let me see..."

"Security matters. I understand." She sounded rather disappointed, though, Hunt thought. Still, when the duke began detailing the deeds of earlier spies and intelligence officers, her interest immediately revived.

Thoughtfully, Hunt swirled the wine in his glass, glancing across the rim at his wife. It occurred to him that he still did not know her as well as he ought. She had told him of her childhood while they were in Derbyshire, relating various scrapes and starts of her youth, but what was she really like now?

Besides curious. He smiled to himself. He had not missed the way she had attempted to ferret information out of the ministers and diplomats last night. And look at her now. As curious as a cat, his Holly was. Perhaps he should caution her against that, especially given the present concerns at the Foreign Office—and her mother's nationality. If she happened to arouse anyone's suspicions, it would do his career no good at all.

After dinner they all went to the theatre and thence to a supper at Lady Mountheath's. When Hunt finally found himself alone with Holly in her chamber, he was almost too tired to remember what he had wanted to say to her. But not quite.

"You seemed to enjoy yourself tonight, my dear," he said casually, as he removed her hairpins.

Holly flashed him a glance. "Yes, I did. The theatre is still a rather novel experience for me, I must admit."

"And last night, as well. I'm gratified to see how well you get on with the ambassadors, in particular." He paused, letting the silky black strands flow through his fingers. "You are becoming quite an asset to me, you know."

She turned to face him fully then, looking so lovely in her sheer nightdress, her hair unbound about her shoulders, that he could barely concentrate on her reply.

"I hope that is true, Hunt. Certainly, I enjoy mingling with such important men—it makes me feel as though I am truly a part of the events shaping the world."

"Yes, well . . . that is as it may be. Still, it will not do for you to become *too* much a part, if you see what I mean." She looked confused, and no wonder. The conversation was not going quite as he had planned. Perhaps he should have waited until morning, when he would be less tired, less . . . distracted.

"What I mean to say—" he tried again, raking his fingers through his own hair and trying not to stare at her smooth, white shoulders "—is that there is such a thing as being *too* friendly, too curious. Especially right now."

Comprehension dawned in her eyes. "Do you mean because of this 'delicate' internal matter?"

"Damn it, Holly! How—?" Hunt sharply reined in his astonishment. "I beg your pardon. But just what *do* you know?"

She shrugged prettily, distracting him again. "Only that there appear to be security concerns. No one would tell me more than that."

"And you shouldn't have been asking." He gave an exasperated sigh. "Very well, I may as well tell you, if only to prevent your trying to worm it out of Castlereagh himself. It appears that there is a security leak in the Foreign Office. Certain confidential information has reached the French during the past week or two—since our arrival back in Town, in fact—which has enabled them to intercept messages that could be detrimental to our negotiations in June. At this point, no one—*no one*—is above suspicion."

"And you are investigating who the leak could be?" she asked eagerly, apparently not the least put off by the seriousness of the situation. She put her hands on his shoulders, her face close to his. "Oh, Hunt, *do* let me help! Please?"

"Absolutely not!" He drew back, aghast. "That would be completely inappropriate, Holly, and possibly danger-ous, as well." He reached for her again.

But she pulled away from him, disappointment plain on her face. "Inappropriate! Honestly, Hunt, at times you sound almost like my sister Blanche. All you think of is the proprieties, while I long for glory, for excitement. Don't you?"

"I find all the glory and excitement I need on the hunt-ing field," he said dryly, willing himself to believe it. He had always fought to suppress the very feelings she called up, trying to satisfy his adventurous tendencies through his ob-session with the hunt. He had to remember, always remem-ber, his responsibilities to the name he bore, responsibilities that his father, Reg, everyone except his grandmother, took so lightly.

"Are you not even trying to find out who it is?" Holly's expression was still clouded.

"Of course I am," he said gently, stepping forward. "We all are. But very cautiously, through time-honoured means. 'Tis safest that way. Can you not see why I wish you well away from it?"

She sighed, apparently capitulating. "I suppose so. But if an opportunity arises where I *may* be of help, you will let me know, will you not?"

In answer, he gathered her into his arms and kissed her thoroughly, then drew her gently towards the blue cano-pied four-poster bed.

Holly went with him willingly.

In the morning, she decided, she would write again to Noel. Perhaps he could shed some light on the mystery. If she could discover the traitor's identity herself, surely Hunt would finally realize how valuable a partner she could be.

CHAPTER FIVE

THREE DAYS LATER, long before she expected to hear from Noel, Holly received a second message. It was delivered by a shabby little street urchin who intercepted her on the front stairs of the house as she and the duchess were returning from a series of morning calls.

"G' day, miladies," he said with an ingratiating smile. "Might ye spare tuppence for a poor starving lad? The *ravens* took me last crumb."

Holly had been about to brush past him as Camilla already had, for she had become somewhat inured to the street beggars by now, but at the sound of Noel's pet name for her, spoken with emphasis by the boy, she paused.

"Perhaps I have a coin or two," she said, opening her reticule. "Do go on inside, your grace. I shall join you in a moment."

Camilla drew her skirts away from the filthy child. "You are too soft-hearted by half, Holly. He'll only take it to some thieving master, I'll be bound. But as you will." She proceeded up the stairs and into the house.

Holly waited until the door had closed behind her before saying, "Did you have something beyond begging in mind, young man?"

The boy gave her a wide grin, his teeth startlingly white against his grimy face. "You are a sharp un, milady! The gennulman's note said 's how you were, and that I's to give this to you." He pulled out a sealed letter addressed to her from among his tattered rags. "Paid me a shillin' m' master did, to deliver it, but I reckon it ain't but a tithe of what he got.'' His eyes gleamed and he gave her a broad wink.

Holly took the hint. "Perhaps another two shillings would be closer to fair." She resisted the urge to tousle the young ruffian's hair, which already stood wildly on end.

"Aye, mum, that'd be fair as fair c'n be." He thrust the letter at her with one hand, and snatched the coins she offered with the other. "Ye c'n find me at the Grey Goose Inn, in the stables, should ye need to send somethin' t' other way. Me name's Peter." Touching a finger to his forehead, he turned and raced off around the corner.

She tucked the letter into her reticule, wondering if the one she'd sent three days ago would reach Noel now that he'd found a more efficient way of communicating with her. No matter. If she received no reply within a reasonable time, she'd simply send another. Tightly clasping her reticule with its precious contents, she went inside.

The duchess had various small duties for Holly to perform, but Holly was finally able to escape to the privacy of her chamber. She simply had to speak to Hunt about finding their own Town house. She knew he did not like the idea of her living alone—and he would be leaving again within a few days, this time for Lisbon—but she was sure she would prefer her own house, be it ever so lonely, to playing companion to Camilla.

But all that would have to wait. For now, she had Noel's letter to occupy her. Making certain the door was locked, she pulled it out of her reticule and broke the seal. As before, it was in their old code, but this time she had no trouble at all deciphering it.

A response to the letter she had sent Noel from Derbyshire, this letter was longer than his first one, and gave her a few more details about his activities in France, though still not so many as she'd have liked. He was working as an under-clerk in one of the government offices there, and already had discovered a few worthwhile tidbits to send on to England, though he did not elaborate.

"The French have apparently made use of the same strategy I have," he wrote then. "Just recently, information has been received here from a clerk in the Foreign Office. If you can do so discreetly, you might wish to warn your new husband, Lord Vandover, about this. Rumour implies that your husband is a man well able to deal with a traitor, or anything else that might arise."

He went on to congratulate her on her marriage and to express his hopes of getting to know Hunt on his eventual return to England. Holly merely scanned those final lines before going back to reread the parts pertaining to the traitor within the Foreign Office. A clerk, Noel said. That would eliminate all the ambassadors and highly placed noblemen from suspicion. At any rate, it gave her a place to start.

She would wait until after Hunt left for Lisbon to begin her own discreet investigation, she decided. That way he would not be made to feel uncomfortable by her inquisitiveness. Holly felt a tiny twinge of guilt at the thought of going behind her husband's back on this, but she subdued it. After all, it was not as though he had actually forbidden her to help him. And how grand it would be if, on his return, she could tell Hunt the name of the man everyone sought. She would be a genuine heroine!

"IT SEEMS I am forever telling you goodbye," said Hunt as he and the duke prepared to depart for Portsmouth a few days later. "We are spending more time apart than together. Pray believe that if I had my choice I would stay."

"I know," replied Holly, reaching up to tenderly touch his cheek. "But I am proud of the work you are doing to bring peace to Europe. I would be a poor patriot indeed were I to attempt to dissuade you from it."

"It makes my going easier to know you will not repine."
He gave her a quick hug. "Indeed, your forbearance is most
heroic."

Holly returned the embrace warmly. She fully intended to
prove herself even more heroic by the time he returned.
"Godspeed, Hunt. I pray your negotiations will go well."

"If they do, I fear it will mean yet another journey for
me, for we hope to arrange a conference between Austria,
Russia and Prussia in June. But it will put us that much
closer to the end of this interminable war."

"Then I promise to be as brave then as I will be now," she
assured him. The end of the war would not only keep Hunt
by her side, it would bring Noel back to England, as well.

He kissed her one last time, fiercely, then hurried out to
the waiting coach.

Holly sighed as it pulled away. She had thought it would
be so exciting to be married to a diplomat, but in fact it was
proving more than a little bit lonely. Then she brightened.

Tomorrow night she and Camilla were to attend a rout
given by Countess Lieven, the Russian ambassador's wife.
Nearly all the members of the Foreign Office who had not
gone to Lisbon would be in attendance. It would be a perfect opportunity for her to begin her enquiries.

That afternoon, while she and the duchess consoled each
other over the temporary loss of their husbands by going out
to buy new bonnets, Holly began to formulate a few discreet questions she might ask some of the clerks.

"FIVE YEARS! Goodness, Mr. Winters, I had no notion
you'd been with the Foreign Office so long." Mr. Winters
was the third clerk she'd managed to speak with thus far, but
Holly had already decided that he was far too beetle-headed
to be any sort of a spy. Indeed, his lack of mental acuity no
doubt accounted for his still being a mere clerk. At any rate,
she was fairly sure the traitor must be a new addition to the
staff.

"Excuse me," she said now, "but I do wish to have a word with my brother-in-law." With a brilliant smile, she left dull Mr. Winters by the potted palm where he stood.

Countess Lieven had outdone herself tonight, Holly thought. Spring flowers were everywhere, jonquils vying with irises in enormous vases. And the buffet that had been spread at one end of the glittering ballroom was the finest she had ever seen. Holly knew that there were a few, the Duchess of Wickburn included, who still raised their eyebrows at their hostess's outspoken passion for the scandalous waltz. Through her influence as patroness, she had managed to introduce it even into Almack's. Tonight there was to be no dancing, however, so the countess's detractors had nothing to complain of.

"Are you enjoying yourself, sister?" asked Lord Reginald as Holly reached his side.

"Indeed, yes," she replied. "And you?"

Reginald grimaced slightly. "'Tis no worse than most of these diplomatic dos, I suppose, but I'd far rather be at the Academy, working on my latest masterpiece. What do you suppose it is that makes ambassadors such deadly bores?"

Holly stifled a giggle, then glanced quickly over her shoulder to be certain none of those "deadly bores" were within earshot. "I vow, you sound like Hunt, though he generally waits for a more private setting to voice such heresy."

"I thank you." He swept her an elaborate bow, setting his numerous watch fobs jingling. "My faith in my own judgement is restored."

She could not suppress a smile. Holly had noticed before that Reginald's attitude towards his half brother was almost one of hero worship rather than the resentment one often saw between siblings. Perhaps the ten-year difference in their ages accounted for it.

" 'Tis not marvellous judgement that prompts you to say such things in an ambassador's own home, however," she pointed out.

"You are right, of course. I shall attempt to improve my outlook with another glass of this excellent champagne. Here is Teasdale—I shall leave him to amuse you until I return."

Holly turned to Lord Reginald's friend with a smile. "Good evening, Mr. Teasdale. I see you were not chosen to carry stacks of paper to Lisbon."

"Thankfully, no. I fear I do not sail especially well," he replied wryly. "It is kind of you, Lady Vandover to go out of your way to make the more insignificant members of the Foreign Office feel less out of place tonight. I have noticed you taking the time to speak with some of the clerks."

"As a newcomer to these circles myself, I can sympathize with them," said Holly, though she glanced rather sharply at her companion. Had he also noticed her careful questioning of his fellows? " 'Tis rather unpleasant to feel oneself an outsider, after all."

"Especially when one longs to be in the thick of things," he returned, startling her. "Pray do not hesitate to tell me I am wrong, but I believe you may have another motive in your assiduous conversation with the clerks tonight."

Holly regarded him doubtfully, hesitating. "As a woman, I am, of course, insatiably curious," she said finally, with an attempt at lightness. "Particularly about subjects which my husband believes do not concern me."

"But I should think they do concern you." His voice was low, but earnest. "You might be of great benefit to the ministry, were you but allowed to act."

This so perfectly coincided with Holly's own opinion that she felt sure that she could trust this man. He was, after all, a friend of Reginald's. "That is precisely what I have told Lord Vandover, on more than one occasion!" she exclaimed. "The traitor might open up to me, a mere woman, where he would never reveal himself to one of his superiors."

Teasdale's eyebrows rose. "Traitor? I had not known the matter was such common knowledge."

"Oh, it is not. I plagued Hunt to death till he told me. But he still would not allow me to help discover the spy's identity."

"And with him away in Lisbon, you mean to prove your worth?" Teasdale guessed.

She nodded. How perceptive this man was! "Already I know that it must be one of the clerks. I received word from . . . a distant cousin in France, implying as much."

"Indeed! You must allow me to assist you in your investigation, then." His smile was warm, but not the least bit improper. "Two may well discover twice as much as one, and as the newest clerk, I am no more likely to arouse suspicion in our traitor than yourself."

"Would you? That would be marvellous! I had wondered—" She broke off. "Here comes Reginald. Please do not mention any of this to him, for he might feel obliged to notify Hunt. I do so wish to surprise him."

"Not a word, on my honour, my lady," Teasdale promised in an undertone just as Reginald joined them. Then, more loudly, "I have not yet paid my respects to the buffet table. If you will excuse me?"

Reginald immediately launched into a detailed description of one of the floral arrangements, which he meant to capture on canvas, but Holly scarcely heard a word. Instead, her thoughts were taken up by dreams of adventure and glory.

DURING THE NEXT TWO WEEKS, Holly was in a fever of impatience waiting for the next gathering where she might expect to see Mr. Teasdale again. Would he have information for her? She had been able to do little on her own, for the duchess had her social calendar scheduled down to the minute.

The only thing Holly had been able to glean, during the course of a morning call with one of the diplomats' wives, was that Mr. Brockman, a clerk she had not yet spoken to, had recently come into a sum of money. The story was that an uncle had left it to him, but she thought it suspicious enough to be worth mentioning to Teasdale.

"Brockman, eh?" he said when she finally imparted that tidbit to him during a reception at the Danish embassy. "I suppose it is possible. He's a quiet fellow, keeps very much to himself. Difficult to get to know, you might say."

"Well, then!" Holly was triumphant. "Does that not settle it?"

"It may. If only..." His voice trailed off thoughtfully. "Do you happen to know which men are acting as liaisons for the final planning meetings for the June talks in Prussia? If Brockman has managed to be named one of the couriers, I believe we'll have our evidence. 'Tis not the sort of thing he would seek, under normal circumstances."

"I'm afraid I don't," she replied, somewhat deflated. "But perhaps I could find out. The duke and my husband have been intimately involved in the planning for those talks. There may well be a list of the names about the house somewhere."

"I would not ask you to pry among their private papers, of course." Teasdale looked faintly shocked. "Still, it would be a coup—for both of us—if we could expose Brockman before Wickburn and Vandover return, would it not?"

Holly lifted her chin. "And so we shall. Of that I am determined."

"You must do whatever seems right to you, of course, Lady Vandover. But now, why do you not go to speak with some of the ladies? 'Twill not do if we are seen talking too long together—we would not wish to arouse Brockman's suspicions."

BEFORE SHE went to bed that night, Holly glanced through the papers on the big desk in the study at Wickburn House. She saw nothing there that appeared to be the sort of list Teasdale had mentioned, however. Then she recalled that Hunt often worked late at night in his own chambers, at the smaller desk he had there. Perhaps that was where he would keep such a list.

Camilla had already retired and Hunt's valet had gone with him to Lisbon, so Holly had no fear of interruption while she searched. Still, she felt more than a bit uncomfortable as she slipped into her husband's chamber. Never before had she been in here without him present.

For a moment, she vividly recalled her last time in this room, on the big, blue-draped bed with Hunt. A sudden longing for him shook her. What a greeting she would give him on his return! She would show him just how much he meant to her. Her eyes grew moist and her breathing rapid as she imagined it.

Reluctantly, she pushed away such thoughts. She felt even more strongly now that she should not be here with Hunt away, poking into his things. For a full two minutes she held an internal debate with herself and finally came to a compromise. She would open no drawers, uncover nothing that wasn't in plain sight. Surely anything left lying about where any servant could see it could not be too secret for her eyes.

Her decision made, she quickly crossed to the desk in the corner. It was littered with papers, but she was careful not to touch them as she examined each one. Most appeared to be unrelated to Hunt's work at the Foreign Office—bills from his tailor, old invitations and such. She was about to give up when she spied the word "Liaisons" at the top of a paper peeping out from beneath a theatre programme.

Almost without thinking, she twitched the programme aside, to reveal a series of names, most of which were known to her. To her disappointment, Mr. Brockman was not among them. Still, she thought, the list might give Teasdale a clue of some sort. Telling herself again that anything left in plain sight could scarcely be considered private, she went to fetch a sheet of paper from her own chamber. Once she had copied the names onto it, she tucked it into the reticule she carried most often. She would give it to Teasdale at the next opportunity.

That opportunity occurred less than a week later, at the theatre. She and Camilla had accompanied Lord and Lady Mountheath, along with a few others whom Holly personally found deadly dull. Reginald was the only person in the party near her own age, but having discovered that Lord Mountheath had once aspired to be a painter, Reggie eagerly recounted his own experiences at the Royal Academy to their host.

The intermission was nearly over when Holly spied Mr. Teasdale. He was surrounded by a group of young bucks who were plainly enjoying themselves immensely, and she wished she might be a part of that group instead. He saw her at the same moment and excused himself from his fellows to greet her.

"Lady Vandover! What a pleasant surprise." Though his voice and demeanour were casual, Holly thought she detected a question in his inflection.

Glancing surreptitiously about, she opened her reticule and pulled the list from it. "Indeed, Mr. Teasdale," she replied gaily, "I did not expect to see you here tonight."

He raised the hand with the list to his lips, palming the paper as he did so. "You grace the theatre with your presence, my lady," he said gallantly. "Perhaps we may speak again later. The curtain will rise in a moment." With an elegant bow, during which the paper somehow disappeared, he took his leave of her.

Holly returned to the duchess and the Mountheaths, feeling both relieved and strangely uncomfortable. Teasdale had behaved as though he had much practice at secreting notes given him in public. Yet she had not particularly thought of him as a ladies' man.

Returning to the box with the others, she attempted to ignore whatever it was that bothered her by telling herself that she was one step closer to discovering the traitor's identity, and proving her abilities to Hunt. He was due back in two weeks' time, if all went well in Lisbon. Surely she and Teasdale would have the answer by then, if not from that list, then from Noel's reply to her queries. She hoped he would not delay in responding.

IN FACT, Noel's letter did not arrive until only three days before Hunt and the duke were expected to return. Several times Holly had to restrain herself from going round to the Grey Goose Inn herself to ask Peter whether something had come for her. She so wanted to surprise Hunt with the traitor's identity!

Teasdale had told her nothing else, though they had encountered each other twice since she gave him the list, so she assumed he had not been able to make use of it. Small wonder, as she had by now convinced herself that those names were likely common knowledge about the Foreign Office. Noel's letter was her last hope. She paid Peter twice what she had last time and hurried directly up to her room to read it, heedless of what the duchess might think.

"I strongly urge you not to pursue this matter alone," Noel began. "Vandover is the man to handle it, and the danger to a woman too great."

Holly nearly crumpled the letter in her frustration, but calmed herself sufficiently to decode the remainder first. She was rewarded for her forbearance.

"Begging you to keep this in mind, I have sought the information you requested, at no small risk to myself, I may add. I hope you find it useful. The traitor is a clerk, as I wrote before, who has but recently obtained his position with the Foreign Office—within the past two months, in fact. I was unable to discover his name, but this clue may enable Vandover to discover who the man is, for he has doubtless launched an investigation already.''

Holly's hands shook as she deciphered these lines. There was only one clerk who had come to the Foreign Office since the beginning of the year, she knew. Teasdale.

As her amazement subsided, she was seized with a thrill of elation. She had done it! She had discovered the identity of the traitor, and without Hunt's assistance. When he returned in three days' time she would tell him—how proud he would be! Perhaps he would even tell his superiors what she had done. She and Noel would be heroes when it all came out!

Then, gradually, doubts began to assail her. Could she reveal Noel's part in this? She had faithfully promised her brother that she would tell no one of his whereabouts. But without this letter, would Hunt even believe her? Teasdale would deny it of course, and she had no idea if any tangible proof might exist. . . .

The list!

For a moment, Holly thought she might swoon. She had given Teasdale that list of names, copied from a document on Hunt's own desk! How could she have been so stupid? But if he still had it, would that not be evidence of his guilt, apart from Noel's letter? Tomorrow night she would see him at an embassy ball. Somehow, she had to discover what he had done with it.

CAMILLA CHATTERED incessantly on the way to the ball, and though the majority of her comments were directed to Reginald, Holly found herself growing impatient. She needed a few moments of silence to plan her attack on Teasdale. Instead she was forced to listen to a recitation of Lady Broadhurst's sins, the chiefest apparently being that she had dared to wear a gown similar to Camilla's to last night's musicale.

The ride was short, and in less than ten minutes the carriage had drawn to a halt outside the Russian embassy. Countess Lieven greeted them at the head of the stairs, just as she had on that fateful night, nearly a month before, when Holly had first taken Teasdale into her confidence.

"And here is my dear Reginald," cooed the countess after exchanging pleasantries with Holly and the duchess. Reginald had become rather the darling of the ambassadorial circle in recent weeks. "Come, I have just obtained a new painting for the front parlour, and I wish to hear your opinion on it."

She led him away, and Camilla, never willing to allow her son long out of her sight, accompanied them, leaving Holly near the door. Before she could gather her thoughts, she saw Teasdale coming towards her. She would simply have to improvise.

"Good evening, Mr. Teasdale," she said brightly, willing her voice to remain steady. He must not guess that she knew. "I am so glad to have this moment to speak to you, for we have been sadly separated by the crowds at other affairs of late."

He stepped close to her. "Ah! You have discovered something, then?" he asked in a low voice.

His expression now struck her as cunning rather than perceptive.

"Indeed, no," she replied hurriedly and was alarmed to hear a faint squeak in her own voice. "I was hoping that perhaps you had discovered something from that list I gave you. Our time is running out."

Teasdale regarded her intently. "As you say. But no, I fear the list gave me no clue as to the traitor's identity."

"A pity. Do...do you still have it?" Holly held her breath.

"I'm afraid not. Did you want it back? I assumed it was merely a copy, so I burned it. It was not a thing that should be allowed into the wrong hands, you know."

For a moment, she wondered if she could have been mistaken. Surely if he were guilty he would show some sign, some hesitancy in his manner? To test him, she said, with certain significance, "I would not wish that to happen, of course. That is why I asked for it." She watched him closely as she spoke, and was rewarded by a flash of comprehension in his eyes. "You cannot blame me for being cautious."

"I blame you? Of course not, dear lady," he replied smoothly. "However, I cannot promise that others would not." He allowed that to sink in for a moment, before saying, with studied casualness, "I became a bit curious about your 'distant cousin' in France, my lady, and made a few enquiries. It appears that the relationship is somewhat closer than you led me to believe."

Desperately, Holly fought to retain her composure. "I cannot imagine what you mean, Mr. Teasdale." Again, her voice showed an alarming tendency to squeak.

"I think you can." He spoke so softly now that she had to strain to hear him over the music and conversation around them. "Your brother is in a perilous position. His continued safety rests entirely in your hands."

"Vandover—" she began.

"Vandover cannot help him, nor would he wish to. And I doubt you would wish him to learn of any of this. Were it discovered that his wife divulged classified information, it would be bad enough. But if it comes out that his own brother-in-law is a traitor, even now on French soil, his diplomatic career would be over and his proud name ruined. And should you feel compelled to tell Vandover, I fear your brother would pay dearly. Do we understand each other?"

Numbly, she nodded.

CHAPTER SIX

"RATHER A ROUGH TRIP but well worth it, eh, Father?"
Hunt tucked his hat under his arm to protect it from the
wind, which blew nearly as briskly in port as it had for the
past week at sea. "Got us home a full day ahead of schedule."

Wickburn nodded rather feebly. Though he was now on
dry land, he still looked a bit peaked. "Worth it," he echoed. "If you say so, son."

Hunt shot a pitying glance at the duke but could not suppress his own high spirits. He'd ached for Holly almost from
the day of their departure. Soon, very soon, he would hold
her in his arms again. Settling his father into the carriage,
he shouted to the coachman to spring the horses.

AFTER AN ENDLESS and perfectly wretched night, during
which she had not slept a wink, Holly had still not come up
with a solution to her predicament. If she remained silent,
she would, in truth, be a traitor herself. But if she told Hunt
about Teasdale, the man might well carry out his threat
against Noel—or even against Hunt himself. What she had
done, however inadvertently, might well destroy her husband's career.

Perhaps, if Hunt were to act quickly enough, before
Teasdale could have an opportunity to send word to anyone about Noel...? But no. She remembered how con-
strained her husband was by the proprieties, always

following the proper channels. Noel might be dead before Teasdale so much as had charges read against him.

And then there was Teasdale's implication that Noel was in fact working for France and not England. Holly did not believe it for a moment, of course, but suppose Teasdale had some sort of falsified evidence? In that case, showing Hunt her brother's letters would be the worst thing she could possibly do. It would lend weight to her enemy's arguments.

On that thought she rose swiftly, determined to do away with that risk, at the least. She should have burned the letters immediately, as Noel had once bade her to do, before his departure. It was mere sentimentality that had led her to keep them, something she could not afford now.

Holly pulled Noel's three letters from their hiding-place beneath the ribbons in her ribbon box and carried them to the hearth. A few embers still glowed in the fireplace, and she set to work with the bellows to coax them to life. After a moment she was satisfied with the result and slowly, reluctantly, picked up the letters—her only link to Noel.

She could not help rereading them before feeding them to the small flame. Would she ever receive another? Not if Teasdale carried out his threat! Steeling herself, she held the first letter to the fire.

It had blackened to ash and she was just thrusting the second letter after it when, unexpectedly, the door to her chamber swung open. To her amazement, Hunt himself stood there.

"You . . . you were not due back until tomorrow," she stammered stupidly, the second letter dangling from her fingers.

"We had good wind the whole way—too good for Father's taste, in fact. Shaved an entire day from the return trip." Smiling broadly, a tender light in his eyes, he came forward, arms outstretched.

Holly rose and took a step towards him, her lips parted, her heart pounding with elation, anticipation—and then alarm. The letters! Swiftly, she flung the last two into the fire, turning back to Hunt even as it blazed up to consume them. "Welcome home, darling." But her first enthusiasm was spoilt, and she feared it showed in her voice.

Indeed, Hunt stopped before touching her. "What is wrong, Holly? What did you just toss into the fire? Some billet-doux from a lover you kept in my absence?" He spoke lightly but his eyes were wary, she thought.

She forced a laugh, though it came out high and brittle. "How absurd you are, my lord! Of course it was no such thing—'twas merely—" she groped for a moment "—merely a note my maid left me yesterday, informing me that a bonnet I ordered was ready. I was...a bit cold, and thought to revive the fire with it."

His wariness deepened to a frown. She could not wonder at it, for her lie sounded incredibly lame even to her own ears. "Holly, is there something you wish to tell me?" He sounded completely serious now, all trace of humour—the humour she had worked to bring into his life—gone as though it had never been.

For a moment, she was sorely tempted to tell him everything. She even opened her lips to say the words, to expose Teasdale as the traitor, before the memory of Noel's face stopped her. No matter what Hunt might think of her, she could not send her beloved brother to his death.

"No," she said flatly. "There is not." All ability for banter, for humour, seemed to have left her, as well.

Hunt's face became a shuttered mask. This must be the very look Lady Anne and the dowager had described to her—the one she had congratulated herself on never having seen.

"Then there is no more to say, I suppose." He nodded curtly. "Pray forgive me for having disturbed you, madam."

Holly sank down on the hearth and stared at the closed door, fighting an overwhelming urge to go after him. But if she did, she knew she would tell him everything and then... She closed her eyes against the tears stinging the lids. Whatever the cost to her, or to her marriage, she could not, *must* not betray Noel.

IT WAS STILL EARLY, but as soon as he had put off his travelling clothes and washed, Hunt went in search of his half brother. As he had expected, Reg was still abed. Though he was undoubtedly glad to see him, Reggie made no secret of the fact that he thought Hunt's greeting could have waited an hour or two.

"If it's an enthusiastic welcome you wanted, you'd have done better to wait until I've had a cup of coffee or two," he said, climbing out of bed to shake Hunt's hand. "Or gone to your wife first, which is what I'd have expected." Hunt winced. "Say! Something wrong there? Why *aren't* you with Holly right now?" Reg demanded of him.

"I'm not sure," Hunt admitted. "That is what I wanted to talk to you about. What precisely has gone on in my absence?"

Though he still looked confused, Reg waved him to a chair. Wrapping himself in a purple brocade dressing-gown, he sat opposite him. "Gone on?" he finally repeated. "Just the usual things you might expect. Routs, balls, the theatre—Mother's hectic social schedule. Diplomatic dos. All a dead bore, of course, but nothing out of the ordinary."

"No, I meant with Holly. She behaved damned peculiarly just now, when I went to her room. And she was burning what looked like a letter. Has she...she hasn't...?"

Reg stared. "Good God, no! She's been friendly and all that is charming to all the old ambassadors and government officials, of course. She always has been. And even if she'd been so inclined—which she hasn't—I can't imagine how she'd have found the time to start up a flirtation. Mother's got her on the go every minute of the day."

Hunt sat back, profoundly relieved. "Thank you, Reg. I didn't believe it—not really—but it's vastly cheering to hear your defence of her. But in that case, what the devil *was* she burning? I never heard so obvious a falsehood in my life as the one she offered when I asked her about it."

"Perhaps some surprise she's planning for you, and you ruined it by returning early," suggested Reg with a shrug. "I don't know. I am sure it will prove to be something perfectly innocent."

"No doubt you are right." Hunt wondered how he could ever have suspected her, even for a moment. "I shall wait, then, until she is ready to tell me of her own accord."

"That's the ticket," Reg agreed. "Likely she'll tell you tonight, or tomorrow at the latest. And now, if that's all, I'll attempt another hour or two of sleep."

Hunt took the hint and left, his heart far lighter than it had been when he came in.

After a hurried breakfast, Hunt and his father left for the Foreign Office to report on the progress of the negotiations. They had gone well, bolstered by Napoléon's renewed threat to much of Europe. In fact, the foreign secretary, Lord Castlereagh, now thought it advisable that Hunt and Wickburn leave to prepare for the June conference in Prussia in no more than two weeks' time.

Though he wanted peace as much as the next man, Hunt mentally cursed this pronouncement. His absences from Holly's side seemed to grow more and more frequent while his visits to England were ever shorter. And this meeting would be too near the fighting to admit any possibility of wives accompanying the diplomats.

The meetings at the Foreign Office went on all day and well into the night. Lord Castlereagh and Lord Palmerston, the secretary of war, questioned Hunt at length about every nuance of the talks in Lisbon. It was clear that the

Duke of Wickburn had little to offer. Thus, though his father made his excuses some hours earlier, it was nearly eleven before Hunt was finally permitted to go.

"Is Lady Vandover at home?" he asked Tilton, as the butler relieved him of his greatcoat and hat in the front hall. On receiving an affirmative response, he hurried up the stairs. It was yet early; surely she had not retired. Perhaps now he could get to the bottom of her little mystery—and enjoy the delights he had been without for far too long.

Anticipation made him forget his weariness as he tapped lightly on her door. "Holly, are you still awake?"

After a long pause, the door opened. "Good evening, Hunt." Her hair was already unbound, much to his disappointment. She was dressed for bed, wrapped tightly in one of her heavier robes, though the evening was fairly warm. "I trust your negotiations went well? I am sorry I neglected to ask before."

She looked anxious, Hunt thought, and more serious than he had ever seen her. Whatever had been bothering her this morning obviously did so still.

"Quite well, thank you," he replied, unconsciously matching the formality of her tone. "Might I come in? I...believe we have a bit of catching up to do." He tried for a humorous, suggestive tone, something she had always responded to in the past. Now, however, there was no answering twinkle in her eyes.

"Of course, my lord," she said quietly, standing aside to let him into the room.

Hunt felt rather at a loss. Any overtures he might make while she was in this mood would seem out of place, almost vulgar. Plainly he would have to determine what had upset her before attempting any kind of seduction.

"Holly, I can see that you are greatly perturbed over something," he began, reaching for her hand. She allowed him to take it, but did not return the clasp. Her hand lay limp in his, and after a moment he released it. "Can you not tell me about it?"

For a bare instant her eyes met his, and he read pain in their green depths before she turned away. "I wish that I could, Hunt . . . but no."

"Is it something I've done?" he asked gently.

Still facing away, she shook her head almost fiercely.

"Then . . . is it something you have done, Holly? Something you now regret?" He braced himself for her answer.

"I—I suppose one might say that," she replied so softly that he had to stoop to hear her. "Certainly I am far from blameless." Then, more strongly, "I am sorry, Hunt, but that is all I can say just now. Please do not press me for more, I beg you."

As frustrated and helpless as he felt in the face of her distress, Hunt could not bring himself to plead with her. He had once begged Camilla to treat him like a son, and it had brought him nothing but scorn. He would not be made a fool of again. Still he made one final effort.

"As you wish," he finally said. "But pray remember that I am here, for the next two weeks at any rate, should you need to talk about whatever it is that is plaguing you. I care, Holly. Remember that."

Her back was still to him, but as he turned to go he heard her voice, so faint that it was almost a whisper. "Thank you."

HUNT DID NOT come to her room again after that night, nor did he make any effort to break through the barrier of reserve that Holly deliberately raised against him. Still, his parting words gave her hope that someday, when this nightmare was over, he would be willing to listen. She prayed that the war might end quickly. Only then would she feel able to confide fully in her husband, to allay his obvious suspicions. She hoped it would not be too late.

The day after Hunt's return, she wrote to warn Noel of Teasdale's threats and to beg him to return to England immediately. She went alone to the Grey Goose Inn, and sought out the boy, Peter, in the stables.

"I have a letter," she told him in an undertone, "to be delivered to the person who wrote to me before. Will five shillings do?"

The lad looked uncomfortable. "Nay, m' lady, two will be plenty," he said.

This struck Holly as rather odd, but she had told Mabel she would be but a moment. "Very well, here are two and here is the letter. Thank you, Peter!"

His discomfort seemed to increase. He glanced around quickly and leaned towards her, as if to whisper something, but at that moment one of the grooms called out to him. "Aye, m' lady," he said gruffly as he turned to resume his duties. "Thank ye."

Strange as this incident was, other thoughts soon pushed it from her mind. Holly had realized on the day of Hunt's return that she would have to maintain a safe emotional distance from her husband if she were to resist telling him everything. In fact, this was not as difficult as she had feared, for Hunt was so involved with preparations for the next meeting that she scarcely saw him.

But now she felt increasingly lonely, despite her own busy schedule. She missed Hunt desperately. As the month of May passed and the time of his next departure drew near, she more and more frequently questioned her decision to remain silent. Whenever she wavered, however, she would remember Noel. Mere marital happiness could not compare to her brother's life.

Yet Holly could not help remembering certain vows she had spoken, on that Christmas Eve that now seemed an age ago, when she was still young, innocent and unscathed by this brutal war of loyalties.

The night before Hunt was to leave for Prussia, a gala farewell event was held at the Foreign Office rooms. For the first time since his return a fortnight since, Holly would be spending an entire evening in her husband's company. This, and the knowledge that he would be leaving again on the morrow made it unusually difficult for her to keep up her pretence of indifference.

"You do not expect to return before July?" asked Reginald, coming up to stand beside them. He glanced sideways at Holly as he spoke, though his question was directed at Hunt. Holly knew that Reginald was curious about their apparent estrangement; she wondered what explanation Hunt had given him for it.

"July at the earliest," Hunt replied. He almost followed Reginald's glance, but seemed to catch himself before he could meet Holly's eye. "So much depends on what Napoléon does next, how far into Prussia he penetrates. If only we could finally unseat him from Spain, the allies might have more faith in us and be willing to grant more concessions."

Reginald held up his hands. "Pray, no more about the wretched negotiations! For this one evening, you are to simply enjoy yourself, brother."

This time Hunt apparently could not resist darting a glance at his wife. Holly flinched away from the desolation in his eyes. This whole situation was so unfair to him! He had respected her wishes by not demanding explanations, though as her husband he had a perfect right to do so. She recalled, too, what the dowager had told her about his childhood. How could she deal Hunt this sort of hurt on top of what he had suffered at his stepmother's hands?

But surely Noel would receive her warning letter any day now, if he had not already. Perhaps, if she could convince Hunt to wait until after his return to launch a formal inquiry against Teasdale . . .

"Vandover!" exclaimed Lady Castlereagh, sweeping over to take Hunt by the arm. "Your father has just been telling me the most outrageous story! You must come listen to it, and you too, Reggie dear, and assure me that it is a complete fabrication. Wickburn can be *so* droll...."

The viscountess led the two gentlemen away. Holly was trying to decide whether to follow when another voice spoke at her elbow.

"A pleasant evening, is it not, Lady Vandover?" Teasdale stood at her side. His smile was charming, and if it held a malicious edge, she doubted anyone else in the room would notice it. "I had rather hoped for a private word with you."

Holly had assiduously avoided Teasdale ever since his vile threats two weeks before and had no desire to speak with him now. "A pity, sir," she said coldly, "for I was just about to follow my husband."

"I believe you can spare me a moment. I have advice you would do well to listen to." Something in his tone made her pause, a chill stealing over her heart.

"Advice?" she asked, striving for a casual tone. "I can't imagine what you mean."

"The letter you attempted to send to your brother. A warning, I presume, though I was unable to decipher the whole."

Her whole body went icy cold. "Then he—"

"He never received it, no," Teasdale finished for her. "And it would be extremely foolhardy for you to attempt such a thing again. Foolhardy for you, and perhaps fatal for your brother—and your husband."

"Hunt?" She tried desperately to control her features. "What has he to do with it?"

"Suffice to say that if I hear the faintest rumour that Lord Vandover is involving himself in the investigation, or shows any particular interest in myself, certain information may find its way into official hands implicating his wife—and, by extension, himself."

"But . . . he was involved in the investigation even before I knew of it!"

"Smile, Lady Vandover. You would not wish anyone to suspect that this is more than an exchange of pleasantries. That is better. You must somehow dissuade him from that involvement. You have until his return from Prussia to decide your best means of doing so."

One of the ambassadors approached them at that moment, and Teasdale bowed deeply to her. "Your servant, my lady," he said more loudly. Nodding deferentially to the ambassador, he went to join the group around the Duke of Wickburn.

CHAPTER SEVEN

THE MONTH OF JUNE was one of anxious waiting, not only for Holly but for all England. Word of Napoléon's triumphs, both on the field of battle and in matters of diplomacy, threw even the gay, frivolous London ton into occasional gloom. Peace was imminent, it was rumoured, but only between France and the rest of Europe—not for Britain. And once Napoléon had all of the Continent under his sway, he would expend all of his energies against Wellington in Spain.

"Are Hunt and Father in any danger, do you think?" Lord Reginald asked Holly anxiously one afternoon as he escorted her and his mother to a modiste's. The duchess had paused to exchange gossip with her friend Lady Mountheath, who seemed as oblivious as she to the general anxiety.

"Not yet, I should think," replied Holly. She was not surprised that her brother-in-law would seek her opinion of the matter. It was common knowledge in the Wickburn household that Holly assiduously read the daily papers for the latest news of the war. Even the servants had been known to ask her about the most recent developments.

"The French seem to have halted their advance at Lützen for the present. Still, Reichenbach is not so very far from there, and if he should—" She broke off, for Lady Mountheath had walked on and the duchess detested hearing talk of the war, though she, like most other fashionable ladies, sported a Prussian helmet cap and military epaulets on her spencer.

"Dear Emma tells me that canary yellow is coming back into fashion," said Camilla gaily, rejoining them. "Isn't it lucky that we have not yet ordered those parasols, Holly?"

Holly managed some suitable reply, her mind still running on the subject she had just been discussing with Reginald. Her close attention to every detail of international events seemed the only thing that kept her sane these days. She had not seen Teasdale again since the night before Hunt left for Prussia, but she had an uneasy feeling that he was watching her every move. She both longed for and dreaded Hunt's return. If only this wretched war would end!

When, on the morning of July 2, Holly read the news of Wellington's resounding victory over the French army in Vittoria, her squeal of delight was loud enough to draw half the household to the breakfast parlour.

"We have driven Napoléon out of Spain!" she cried exultantly, to the delight of the assembled. "The war is over, praise God!" Tears of joy streamed down her face.

Amidst the babble of excited voices, she heard, in the distance, a faint booming. They all rushed to the window in time to see fireworks, faint against the morning sky, going up in the direction of Carlton House.

All that day and the next, London took on the aspect of one huge celebration. The Spanish consul threw a magnificent ball on unbelievably short notice and, on their way there, Holly marvelled at the profusion of coloured lanterns and gay banners, proclaiming *Wellington and Victory*, and *Victory, June 21, 1813!*

By now, though, she had realized that this victory, though highly significant, did not in fact signal the end of hostilities with France. Napoléon yet retained a firm grip on much of Prussia and the eastern portion of the Continent. Still, she could not completely resist the wild enthusiasm that gripped London, however unresolved her own problems might be.

At the Spanish consulate, spirits were especially high. Champagne flowed freely and the orchestra's music took on a note almost of hysteria. Through a dreamlike blur of contagious euphoria, Holly looked up to see her husband and the Duke of Wickburn bearing down on them.

"They told us at Wickburn House that you were here," said the duke to his wife, kissing her soundly. "We came at once to help you to celebrate."

Holly smiled up at Hunt, for the moment conscious only of her pleasure at seeing him again. He searched her face for a moment, then swiftly bent to kiss her. She responded without thinking, clinging to him as almost-forgotten sensations sprang up within her. Hunt tightened his grasp briefly but then released her, apparently aware once more of their surroundings.

He glanced over at Reginald as he called out an enthusiastic greeting and Holly, only mildly embarrassed, looked around to see if many people had witnessed their embrace. Then her throat closed as, over Hunt's shoulder, she saw the thin, clever face of Mr. Teasdale regarding her knowingly. All his threats came flooding back. Her dismay must have shown on her face, for he held her gaze for a moment, then smiled in apparent satisfaction.

That silent exchange with Teasdale spoiled the evening for Holly. When Hunt turned back to her after a few minutes of conversation with his brother, she couldn't help behaving coolly towards him, as she had during his last, brief visit to England. He seemed to sense the change in her at once, visibly cooling himself. Though she ached to smile at him again, to invite another kiss, to be his wife fully once more, the chilling knowledge of Teasdale's watchful eyes restrained her.

While all of London celebrated around her, Holly felt more miserable than ever.

THE DUKE OF WICKBURN and his family were among the last of the ton to leave London. One morning in late July, Holly found herself having a rare, brief moment alone with Hunt in the breakfast room. Gazing across at him as he read from a stack of papers, she felt suddenly shy. It had been months now since they had even engaged in conversation.

With her eyes she traced the strong curve of his jawline, the careless fall of golden brown hair that she had once stroked so lovingly. A surge of longing seized her. Had it really been necessary that she push him this far away?

Quickly, before she could reconsider, she asked, "Have you given any thought, my lord, to going up to Wickburn in advance of your parents?" It was not quite what she had meant to say, nor had she intended her voice to sound so cool. She held her breath.

He sought her gaze across the table for a brief moment, and then looked back to his papers. "In fact, I have." Holly's heart began to flutter, but his next words dashed her faint hope. "I leave in two days' time and will reach Wickburn on Friday. There is a matter I wish to attend to with the steward before the rest of the family arrive the following week."

"Oh, but—" What could she say? That she wanted to come with him? He would want to know why. And if she told him the truth—that she missed him and wanted to spend time with him—he might, quite reasonably, ask for an explanation for her long silence. An explanation she did not yet dare to give him.

But her need for him was now so great that she tried again. "I rather wished to go to Wickburn early myself." To her surprise her voice was perfectly steady.

His look this time was unreadable. "Had you told me sooner, I could have arranged for you to accompany me. As it is, I have already made all the travel plans. Nor would Camilla thank me for disrupting her social schedule."

He referred, Holly knew, to the final flurry of engagements to which the duchess had already committed, including a farewell dinner at Wickburn House. Hunt, apparently, intended to miss it. At that moment, the duchess herself breezed in.

"Holly, are you still sitting over your breakfast? You have not forgotten that we are expected at Lady Southwark's within the hour, have you?" She flashed a polite, insincere smile at Hunt. "Your father wishes your presence in the library," she informed him. "Something about the steward."

AFTER THE SIXTH STOP in as many hours, Holly began to fully understand Hunt's reluctance to travel with his stepmother. At the rate they were going, they would be fortunate to reach Wickburn in four days, she thought, rather than the two it would have taken her and Hunt alone. The duchess was apparently incapable of passing an inn without ordering the carriages to a halt.

"Mama, I thought you wanted to reach Bedford by nightfall," complained Reggie as they resumed their places in the luxurious travelling coach. "At this rate, we'll be lucky to make Shefford."

The duke had elected to ride for the next stage of the journey, an option Holly envied, though it was rather a relief to be spared Wickburn's attempts at wit for a while. Reggie was no horseman, which accounted for his presence in the coach, but he apparently relished his mother's style of travelling no more than did Hunt.

"Nonsense, my love," responded the duchess placidly. "I have made this trip dozens of times and have always reached Bedford. The inn at Shefford rarely has clean sheets and the breakfasts are deplorable, so we will certainly not stay the night there."

Reginald settled down for yet another nap, of which he seemed capable of an interminable number, and Holly turned her attention out the window, hoping to discourage more aimless chatter in Camilla's execrable French or Italian. She seemed to regard Holly as her private language tutor, though she never showed the slightest inclination to improve her appalling accent, however good an example Holly set her.

When the carriage drove through the gates at Wickburn late on the afternoon of the fifth day, Holly was heartily sick of travel in general and of the duchess in particular. Her head ached abominably, and every bone in her body felt stiff and sore from spending so many days cramped into one position. At the sight of the imposing mansion her spirits revived. She had been so happy here last winter. Surely in this setting, she could restore a measure of intimacy to her marriage.

To her disappointment, Hunt was not on hand to greet them on their arrival, although Duchess Aileen was.

"Made a five-day trip of it again, did you?" she called from the top step as Reginald handed his mother and Holly from the coach. The duke was already up the stairs, saluting his mother's cheek with a kiss.

"You know how Camilla travels, Mother," he said with a chuckle. "Nary an inn must go to waste; illness may result from haste."

"Aye, I know," replied the dowager, but her smile was warm. "Hunt is hereabouts somewhere—down at the kennels, I believe." Though she spoke to them all, the dowager's eye, catching Holly's, was questioning. Had Hunt told her something?

"We'll send one of the servants down to fetch him presently," said the duchess before Holly could suggest going to him at once. "First we must all go in and freshen up, and perhaps have a rest. Travelling is so *exhausting*." She assumed her die-away air and the duke was instantly at her side.

"Of course, my love. Come, I'll help you upstairs."

When Holly hesitated, Camilla beckoned to her. "Come along, my dear. You will wish to change your gown at once, I know." Though she would have preferred to join Hunt in the kennels, Holly obediently followed her inside, all the while silently deriding herself for her lack of courage.

The dowager watched Holly as she followed Camilla upstairs, a frown creasing her brow. So! She had not imagined the constraint in Hunt's manner. And the trouble apparently concerned his wife. What could have happened during the London Season to sour what had looked like a most promising marriage? She meant to find out.

Counting to one hundred to give the others time to reach their chambers, the dowager rang the bell. "Fetch Vandover from the kennels, Thomas," she told the footman who appeared. He bowed and left. If Hunt were not forthcoming with information, she would try her hand with Holly. And after that, there was always Reginald. He might know what was going on.

After a few minutes Hunt entered the parlour, though he declined to sit. "I'm covered in dirt, Grandmama," he said, leaning against the mantelpiece. "You wanted me?"

"Your wife returned home fifteen minutes ago," she informed him. "I was surprised you did not see fit to greet her."

As she had expected, Hunt stiffened. "Nor did I perceive her seeking me the moment she arrived. I will see her soon enough." His grandmother knew him well enough to sense the pain beneath his show of irritation.

"What is it, Hunt? What has happened between you?"

His features appeared to be chiseled from marble. "Happened? Nothing has happened, madam. Not for quite some time."

The dowager blinked. "I see." She allowed a quaver to enter her voice. "Then I am not to see my great-grandson before I die?" One corner of Hunt's mouth twitched, but she could not tell whether with amusement or annoyance.

"You seemed so happy together after the wedding...." She let the statement hang in the air between them.

"Yes. Yes, we did." To her disappointment, her grandson did not elaborate. "If you will excuse me, Grandmama, I should like to change out of these breeches before dinner." With an abrupt bow, he left her.

"Fiddlesticks," she muttered.

Hunt reached the top of the staircase before it occurred to him that Holly was probably in her own rooms, which of course adjoined his. He paused. Perhaps he should have waited until she quitted them before coming up. If he went into his chamber now, she would surely hear him.

Then, with a snort, he strode on down the corridor. What did it matter? If past events were any indication, she was unlikely to say or do anything about it. It had been a long time since she had deliberately sought out his company. His mere presence in the next room was unlikely to disrupt her toilette.

He was just passing her door when an unbidden image came to his mind—a vision of what she might look like at that moment, perhaps partially disrobed as she changed for dinner. With a will of its own, his hand strayed towards the handle of her door. He snatched it back quickly.

No! She was the one who had withdrawn from their marriage. Closing himself off from her, from the feelings she had once awakened in him, was mere self-defence on his part. And she apparently preferred it that way.

Once, Reg had commented on Holly's aloofness within Camilla's hearing. His stepmother had immediately hinted that Frenchwomen were not known for their fidelity. Hunt refused to believe that—and Reg had assured him it was impossible. But Holly was hiding something. Her look, her whole demeanour told him so. Ever since that morning in May, she had been unable to meet his eye directly.

But she had repulsed his offer of help, and he had decided then that Holly must make the first move towards reconciliation. His pride, his honour, demanded it. Still, as he entered his own rooms, it occurred to him that pride and honour made for damned cold companions, especially at night.

HOLLY'S FINGERS FROZE in the act of tying the ribbons at her neckline when she heard the familiar firm footstep in the hallway. He had come. But the footsteps continued on past her rooms, and a moment later the door to Hunt's chambers opened and closed.

"Thank you, Mabel, that will be all," she said to her maid, who was pinning up a loose curl. Pressing her lips tight together to keep them from trembling, Holly rose and walked over quickly to open her door. She could not suppress one glance in the direction of Hunt's door before turning towards the stairs.

The dowager was waiting in the parlour when she entered. "My, you managed to transform yourself quickly, my dear," she said, patting the sofa beside her. "Come, sit down, do. I think we need to talk."

Wondering again what Hunt had said to his grandmother, Holly moved slowly to take the seat indicated. "Talk, your grace?" she asked warily.

"Talk," repeated the dowager. "And have you forgotten how to call me Grandmama, as you used to do? Hunt will tell me nothing, but I know things are not as they ought to be between you. I should like to help if I can."

Holly was already shaking her head. She had missed the dowager even more than her own mother, but she dared not confide in her, especially now she knew Hunt had not. "We merely seem to have grown apart. Once we have got over the rough spots of marriage, we will no doubt rub along well enough."

The dowager's eyes gleamed. "Rough spots, you say? And what might those be?"

"The demands of Society, of his diplomatic duties, different friends, different interests," Holly improvised quickly, wishing with all her heart she could unburden herself to this old woman who truly seemed to care. "And he has been away so much, we . . . have scarcely had time to get to know each other."

"Different friends?" asked the dowager sharply. "Hunt has not taken another mistress already, has he?"

Holly could feel the colour leaving her face. She had not even considered that possibility before. "I—I really do not know," she said finally. "I don't think so."

"And you? It isn't at all the thing to be pursuing lovers before begetting an heir, you know, lass."

Such plain speaking went beyond anything Holly had expected—even from the blunt dowager. With an effort, she closed her gaping mouth and swallowed before answering. "I've done no such thing, I assure you! A few men have flirted with me, of course," she admitted, in case the dowager should question Reginald or the duchess, "but it was very innocent and I never gave any of them the least encouragement."

Her cheeks were burning, and she feared that the dowager might misinterpret that as a sign of guilt, but the perceptive old lady nodded, apparently satisfied.

"Glad to hear it. In that case, I'm sure whatever's come between you can be got over. Stands to reason you don't know each other too well, what with such a short courtship and then Hunt off gallivanting over the Continent ever since the wedding." She snorted. "Camilla is doing her damnedest to keep you apart, too, I'll be bound. Well, I'll do my best to put a stop to *that* while you're here. But the rest is up to you." She nodded again.

Holly wished it could be that easy.

HER FIRST SIGHT of Hunt was across the dinner table that evening. Though she'd only been apart from him a week, she was almost astonished at how handsome he appeared. And how cool. Was this really the man she had married? He seemed almost a stranger.

Once, she caught his eyes upon her, and she ventured a tentative smile. He did not return the smile, but neither did he immediately turn away. It was a start, though to what she could not say.

After dinner, Hunt and his father stayed closeted together in the library until bedtime—long past the time Holly reluctantly followed the duchess upstairs. Though she tried to stay awake until he came up, her eyes drifted closed and the next thing she knew it was morning.

It was, in fact, a perfectly glorious morning. The sun was coaxing fragrance from grass, leaves and flowers to linger on the light breeze. After a hurried, solitary breakfast, Holly stepped outdoors to enjoy it. Standing on the top step, she breathed deeply of the mingled perfume of summer. She had missed the country!

As neither the duchess nor the dowager had yet arisen to order her day, Holly decided to explore the grounds. She and Hunt had done so before their marriage, but the rich emerald grass and deeper greens of fully clothed oaks and maples made it a different place entirely. Still, she found herself noting similarities, and soon her feet led her in the direction of the kennels.

Not until she had entered the building did Holly admit to herself that she had hoped to find Hunt there. But she refused to brood, instead hurrying forward to greet the animals. One or two hounds in particular seemed ecstatic to see her, nearly climbing the gate in their delight.

Startled, she looked closer. "Belltongue? Saddleback?" Certainly the dog on the right possessed the same black marking across his back that had inspired his name.

At her words, the pair began to whimper and whine, shoving the other hounds aside to get their cold black noses into her hand.

"It *is* you! But how ever...?" Of course—Hunt must have done it. He must have stopped in Derbyshire, at Mr. Danvers's farm, on his way here last week and purchased them. Scanning the rest, Holly thought she recognized four others of her father's old pack, though they did not respond to her the way her two favourites did.

After a happy half-hour spent crooning to the hounds, Holly headed back to the house, determined to thank Hunt for buying them. He had to have done it for her. Surely that was proof that his affection was not entirely extinguished, that their marriage still had a chance.

Perhaps here, at Wickburn, she could risk telling him the truth. Teasdale was not watching her now. Surely together they could come up with some way of foiling his plans. Whatever the danger, she knew she could not endure this estrangement much longer.

On entering the house, she was informed by Deeds that the duke and his son were again in the library, where they conducted most of the estate business. Thanking the butler, Holly approached that room's double doors, which had been opened to take advantage of the fresh summer breeze circulating throughout the mansion.

"...don't have the resources to investigate every single rumour." Hunt sounded angry and Holly paused, unwilling to interrupt what might be an argument.

"But we cannot afford to take chances." The duke's voice was peevish. "You are one of three men eligible for a top ministry position. Even the slightest breath of suspicion would remove your name from consideration. Perhaps you should ask her to make a complete deposition, denying any correspondence with the French."

"Of course I will ask her to do no such thing. Holly is no more a spy than you are, Father. Just because her mother is French—"

Dismayed, Holly backed away. They were talking about her! Fighting down a choking surge of panic, she hurried for the stairs.

CHAPTER EIGHT

She could never tell Hunt the truth now, Holly realized. With his strict code of honour, even if he agreed to remain silent for Noel's sake he would never accept the post once he knew what she had done. She would *not* allow Hunt to sacrifice his career because of her stupidity. No, no matter what it cost her, she had to remain silent awhile longer.

Half blinded by tears of frustration as she reached the head of the broad, curving staircase, Holly ran headlong into the dowager.

"Oh! My pardon, Duchess Aileen," she exclaimed, reaching out to steady the old woman. "I—I was not watching where I was going, I fear."

The dowager peered closely at her, but only said, "No harm done, child. Indeed, I was hoping to run into you this morning." She chuckled. "Though not quite so literally, I must admit. I thought you might care to drive with me round the cottages today."

"Certainly." Holly grasped at any excuse to be away from the house. "Have you baskets to deliver?"

The dowager nodded. "Aye, I've had them made up for some time, but 'tis not as easy as it used to be for me to get about, I fear. An active companion will make the task more pleasant, and quicker, too."

Her hearty cheerfulness soothed Holly's jangled nerves. She was able to smile. "I find myself praying, ma'am, that I will be half so active as you when I reach your age. Can you not arrange for one of the servants to make the deliveries when none of the family are here?''

"Oh, I do. Necessities are sent out weekly, but I like to visit in person when I may. A servant cannot be trusted to notice the needs that proud people will not mention. And some of our tenants are very proud, indeed, despite their poverty.''

Even in London, Holly had heard that famine threatened much of England, but there, it had been the subject of political discussions on policy. Now she began to understand the human element involved.

"Your tenants are very fortunate to have you,'' she told the dowager sincerely as she followed her down to the pantries, where the prepared baskets were ranged on a shelf.

"I hope they remain fortunate after I am gone.'' Her voice was full of meaning and Holly understood. It would be her responsibility to see to the needs of the tenants then, as Camilla ignored their very existence.

"I will make every effort to see that they do,'' she promised softly, praying that she would be allowed to do so once Hunt knew the truth.

The dowager gave her a quick hug. "Thank you, my dear. I knew that you would.''

"But pray do not leave us too soon, Grandmama,'' Holly blurted out, seized by a sudden fear that the dowager's concern stemmed from more than advancing age. "Not only the tenants would be devastated by your absence, I assure you!'' She felt shaken at the thought of losing this old woman who had come to mean so much to her.

The dowager merely smiled, turning back to the shelves to point out the baskets to the footman waiting to carry them out to the carriage.

Holly's respect for the dowager rose even higher during the course of that day, as did her desire to emulate her. It was borne in upon her that a woman's role could extend far beyond that of wife and mother. A rewarding existence need not depend on a husband's companionship—or even his love.

Oddly, just as this realization strengthened Holly's resolve to remain silent for his sake, Hunt's manner towards her began to thaw noticeably. He still spent his evenings closeted with the duke and his days riding about the estate, but during his few free hours at home he did not attempt to avoid her. In fact, the very morning after she overheard those disturbing words in the library, he joined her at the breakfast table.

"Beautiful weather, is it not?" he asked casually while filling his plate. His back was to her, but there was no one else in the room. "If it holds, I may persuade a few of the local fellows to some cub hunting. Give the hounds an early start on their training."

It was scarcely a loverlike speech, but it was something. Holly swallowed nervously, unsure after what she had heard yesterday whether she would be wise to attempt any kind of a reconciliation. Her heart paid little attention to such reasoning, however, fluttering giddily in her breast.

"I was down at the kennels yesterday looking at the hounds," she said, her eyes on her creamed sole. "Thank you for purchasing part of my father's pack." Her words sounded blunt even to her own ears. They were not the ones she had framed on her way back to the house yesterday, but at least she had thanked him. Timidly, she risked a glance in his direction to find him half smiling.

"Did I choose the right ones? I thought I recalled you mentioning a Saddleback and Bell-something." His eyes searched hers, asking a different question—one she was not yet ready to answer. She dropped her gaze again.

"Yes. Saddleback and Belltongue. They were my special pets, though Father always discouraged me paying too much attention to them. They...they knew me at once."

"They seem to be fine animals, and Danvers assured me they hunted well last season. Saddleback, particularly, should make a splendid stallion hound, as well."

Holly could not bring herself to meet Hunt's eyes. Suddenly, she wished she had not overheard his conversation with the duke yesterday. Then she would be eagerly following up his peace overture instead of sitting here like a lump, afraid to take the discussion away from the hounds.

"Yes, Saddleback comes of excellent stock, out of Regina by Silvertone."

"Silvertone? Was that Silvertone '09?"

She nodded, risking a quick peek at him. His eyes shone, but not precisely at her.

"Why, that hound is practically a legend!" he exclaimed. "Danvers must not have realized it, or he'd have charged me four times what I paid. He never even mentioned their sires, in fact, now that I think on it."

Holly felt a small glow. Hunt must not have asked then; further evidence that he had bought the hounds solely in an attempt to please her. She was glad that he felt he had made a good bargain on the purchase.

"Do you happen to know who Belltongue's sire was?" he asked.

She was cataloguing Belltongue's parentage, as well as that of the other hounds he had bought, when Reginald sauntered in.

"Don't tell me he's already got you doting on those smelly beasts, too?" he asked Holly in mock horror when he understood the tenor of their conversation. "I can't abide the things, or the sport, neither. Surely there must be a more efficient way to rid the countryside of foxes."

During the friendly debate that followed on the merits of fox-hunting, obviously only the latest in a series extending back several years, Holly slipped away. She and Hunt appeared to be on friendly footing again, for which she was grateful. But she was not yet certain how close she could afford to let him get.

Watching her leave, Hunt lost the thread of his discussion with Reg as he thought over their conversation—the first they'd enjoyed in months. His brother noticed his abstraction at once.

"Have things still not ironed themselves out?" he asked sympathetically, letting the other subject drop. "She seemed friendly enough towards you just now."

Hunt shrugged noncommittally. "She was willing to answer my questions about the foxhounds, at least. I haven't dared ask her any others."

"So you still have no idea what caused this change in her? She seemed happy enough when—" Reg broke off in evident embarrassment, which Hunt had no difficulty interpreting.

"When I was away?" he finished bitterly. "It does appear that I am the problem, does it not?"

Reg looked uncomfortable. "Well, it *was* upon your return from Lisbon last May that she first began to behave strangely. And then again, when you came back from Prussia... Are you certain you've done nothing to...to hurt or frighten her, Hunt? She really is rather a remarkable woman. I'd hate to think—"

"So I am to be the villain of the piece, am I?" Hunt tried to force a laugh, but the sound that came out was strangled. "My *remarkable* wife is incapable of anything blameworthy?" He stopped short of telling Reg that she had all but admitted her culpability the one time he had questioned her.

"Come now, Hunt, you know I didn't mean it that way. But as I told you when you first asked, I can't think what she could have done. I mean, Mother kept her busy every moment in London. Did she never tell you what the paper was she was burning?"

Hunt shook his head.

"Why not just ask her, then?" asked Reg practically.

"She requested that I not try to force her confidence, and I gave my word," he replied curtly.

"You and your blasted honour!" Reg was plainly exasperated. "You cannot treat a woman as you would a man. It could be she's dying for you to ask again."

"Do you think so?" Hunt was struck by this idea. "If the opportunity arises, I could at least throw out a hint, I suppose."

Reg clapped him on the back. "A capital notion, Brother! It will do my heart good—and Grandmama's, too—to see you two behaving like lovebirds again."

AMIDST THE BEAUTIFUL, nostalgic surroundings of Wickburn, Holly found it all too easy to forget the gulf she had deliberately created between Hunt and herself. Instead, she kept recalling those idyllic early days of their marriage, when life had held such promise, such laughter. She had to force herself to remember the danger that threatened; a danger that now seemed remote, belonging only to London.

Holly recognized the hazard this sort of thinking posed. It would be too easy to allow emotion to cloud her judgement. Until she gained better control over her response to Hunt, she reluctantly decided it would still be wise to give her husband a wide berth.

Hunt, however, seemed less willing than before to let her do so. He engaged her again in conversation at breakfast the next two mornings, and in the parlour before dinner the evening after that. The topics were impersonal, but more and more frequently the looks she noticed in his eyes were not.

On that particular night, as she undressed for bed, Holly felt a sudden premonition that he might come to her room, though he had not done so for more than two months now.

"Leave my hair as it is, Mabel," she said to her maid on impulse. "I believe I shall sit up and read by the candle for a bit, and would prefer it out of my face. I can brush it out myself before I get into bed."

She could tell by Mabel's knowing look that the maid knew what she was about, but she didn't care. By now, Hunt's continued absence from her bedchamber was likely creating more gossip belowstairs than his presence would. She settled herself in an armchair with a new novel, nervously awaiting the sound of her husband's footsteps.

"FATHER, my eyes are beginning to cross." Hunt yawned conspicuously. "I see no reason we cannot finish going over these figures tomorrow."

"I suppose so," replied the duke, standing to stretch. "I don't know why Camilla insists on my leaving this till after dinner, anyway. Waste of candles. Make more sense to do this sort of thing during daylight hours, but she won't have it. Wants me there while she sits for that portrait Reg is doing of her."

"So that's where you've been disappearing to." Hunt chuckled. "Well, tonight Camilla can have you all to herself. I'm off to bed." He rose.

The duke bade him good-night, then sat back down himself and poured another measure of brandy. Somehow, he didn't think Camilla would be pleased to have him come up to bed early. No sense risking it. He took a satisfying sip of the stuff, the best his cellars had to offer.

Hunt, meanwhile, mounted the stairs with a sense of anticipation. He was not particularly fatigued, but it had been a plausible excuse to get away from a tedious task. And he had reason tonight to wish to go to bed earlier than had been his habit lately.

He went first to his own rooms and quickly divested himself of his neckcloth and coat without ringing for his valet.

Then, without giving himself time to think or reconsider, he tapped lightly on the dressing-room door.

"Come in." Holly's voice sounded as quiet and composed as she appeared to be when he entered her boudoir. She sat at her ease, a book in her hands and a single candle burning beside her. Looking up at him, she smiled. "Good evening, my lord."

Hunt paused for a moment, drinking in the sight of her—soft and feminine in her lilac silk wrapper, her hair still piled high on her head. The significance of that detail penetrated his rush of desire—she had been expecting him.

"Good evening, my lady." Though his voice was steady he trembled with his need for her. Gone was his half-formed intention of requesting another explanation of the note she had burned back in London, so long ago it now seemed. "I thought you might require some assistance in unpinning your hair."

Holly stood, her sweet curves outlined in shimmering lavender. "Yes, I do, as a matter of fact." She took a tentative step towards him. "I was hoping you would come."

He closed the distance between them in two long strides, and she came willingly into his arms. Hungrily, he sought her lips, revelling in her eager response. Her hair forgotten, he guided her to the bed.

Their lovemaking was passionate but brief, for Hunt found himself unable to go slowly. Only when he lay sated for the first time in more than three months did he finally remember the matter that lay between them. Though he hated to disturb the fragile truce they had achieved, he had to try.

"Holly, I have missed you."

"And I, you, Hunt," she replied softly. He imagined that she was smiling, though in the dimness it was impossible to be sure.

Steeling himself against the wave of tenderness that swept through him, he made himself ask, "Why have we been such strangers to each other, my sweet? What is it you are hiding?"

She stiffened at once in his arms, though her voice was still soft when it finally came. "Pray do not ask me that, Hunt, not yet. You . . . you said that you would not. . . ."

Mentally he cursed Reg for persuading him to break his word. But his self-condemnation warred with irritation and a sense of betrayal that she would not confide in him even now.

"I am trying to be patient, Holly, but all this secrecy seems very unnatural to me. As your husband, I have a right to know—" he broke off, striving to subdue the bitterness in his tone "—to know about anything that is troubling you."

She shifted beside him, turning away. "I know you do. You could . . . you could demand the truth, even beat it out of me, and still be perfectly within your rights."

Pain and shock turned his voice cold. "I am sorry that you should think me capable of such a thing. I said before that I was willing to listen whenever you were ready to talk. Plainly you do not trust me enough to do that."

He sat up, groping for his breeches. "I must apologize for breaking my word. Pray believe that it was concern for you that led me to do so. I will not make that mistake again." Ignoring her soft gasp of protest, he pulled on his buckskins, draped his shirt over his shoulders and left the room.

THE NEXT MORNING, Holly received a tersely worded note on her breakfast tray. Hunt was going into the Shires to cub hunt for the next few weeks. He had intimated to her before that he intended to train the young hounds primarily on Wickburn lands, but he had apparently changed his mind. Already, he had "walked" this year's pups to local farmers rather than going farther afield as he might have. She knew that this sudden decision must be the result of her refusal to confide in him last night.

She had come so close to doing so! Had he coaxed her but a little bit more, she would have relented and told all. She had known it at the time, and intentionally said what she knew would hurt him, though it nearly broke her heart to do so. And instead of coaxing, he had turned cold and left her—just as she had intended.

Holly crushed the note, feeling the stiff corners of the paper cutting into her palm. Perhaps it was just as well that Hunt would be gone for a while. After last night, she needed time to prepare fresh defences for her heart if she were to remain silent. She had to keep Hunt's career—and Noel's life—safe a while longer.

STILL, IT WAS with a renewed sense of hope that Holly tackled the tasks the dowager set her over the next two weeks. Feeling needed was a wonderful tonic for depression, she found. August was well advanced and harvest, meagre as it was, under way when Hunt finally returned. Coming back from visiting a family whose cottage had burned to the ground two days previously, she saw his cloak hanging on a hook by the kitchen door.

Pausing only to wash her hands, she hurried upstairs to greet him. On reaching the front parlour, she found him already in conversation with the duke. The duchess, the dowager and Reginald looked on in evident concern.

"Very serious indeed," the duke was saying. "Had you not come back today, I'd have sent someone after you."

"What is it?" Holly interrupted precipitately. "Has there been an accident? Is someone hurt?" Fresh from the sad ruins from that fire, she thought first of the tenants.

Hunt turned to face her, but his thoughts were clearly elsewhere. Neither warmth nor coldness showed in his expression. "Not precisely," he said shortly. "There have been disturbing developments in London, and Father and I must be off at once."

"Yes, I suppose that would be best," said the duke, plainly relieved to have Hunt here to make the decision for him. He turned to his wife. "My dear, I must take my leave of you, I fear, but you will join me in Town for the Little Season, will you not?"

"Of course." She came forward to kiss him on the cheek, flicking a glance in Holly's direction. "Let me ring for one of the maids to help your man pack."

"Is there anything I can do?" Holly asked, curiosity warring with disappointment.

Hunt finally seemed to really see her. "Certainly," he replied. "You may tell Cook to prepare a hamper for us to take. That way we'll only have to stop to change horses. We can get several hours behind us before nightfall."

"But what—" she began.

He shook his head. "I'm sorry, Holly. We are not at liberty to discuss what has happened—with any of you." He smiled then, and a trickle of warmth stole through her.

Hoping that her own smile told Hunt what was in her heart, she hurried to do his bidding.

CHAPTER NINE

DURING THE RETURN TRIP to London, Holly almost welcomed Camilla's inconsequential chatter, as it prevented her from dwelling on her own thoughts. Still, there were occasional lulls during which she wondered what matter had taken Hunt so suddenly to Town—and whether it had anything to do with Teasdale or Noel.

As there was no way she could discover the truth until they reached London, she put the subject from her mind, determinedly engaging the duchess and Reginald in desultory conversation once again. She even went so far as to spend the final day of travel voluntarily attempting to expand her mother-in-law's limited French vocabulary.

During the pomp and bustle that greeted their arrival at Wickburn House, Holly wished again that she and Hunt needn't share a house with his parents. Hunt had spoken of no more lengthy diplomatic journeys. Why should it not now be possible for them to set up their own household elsewhere? If the opportunity arose, she would ask him about it.

Just now, though, he was not present. He and the duke, they had been informed by Tilton, had left early for the Foreign Office and, if they followed recent precedent, would not return until late. She had, perforce, to turn her mind to other matters. That proved far easier than she had expected.

"Oh, my dear, I am far too exhausted to deal with these just now," said Camilla, waving at the huge stack of correspondence that awaited them on the escritoire in the drawing-room. "Would you be an angel and sort through them for me? Doubtless you can handle the responses to all but a few. Just set aside any that require my personal attention." With that, she rang to have tea and a tray delivered to her chambers and allowed Reginald to escort her upstairs.

With the duchess's abdication, Holly found she had other responsibilities, as well, including consultations with the cook and housekeeper. She blessed the dowager again for her invaluable tutelage on such matters. Finally she turned to the mountain of correspondence and began to sift through it. Though disappointed, she was not particularly surprised to find nothing from Noel in the stack. Presumably if Teasdale could intercept her letters to him, he would similarly prevent Noel's from reaching her. With a sigh, she opened the first invitation in the pile.

True to Tilton's prediction, the duke and marquess did not return until nearly midnight. Holly stayed downstairs answering letters and invitations, in hopes that she and Hunt might have an opportunity to talk. At the very least, she wanted him to know she cared enough to wait up for him. She had made it more than halfway through the stack when she heard the front door open.

"Good evening, my dear," said Hunt cordially, coming in with his father. Though he kissed her cheek in welcome, his expression was troubled and tired. "I trust your journey was not too fatiguing?"

"Not at all," she lied, longing to fling herself into his arms but acutely conscious of the duke's presence.

"Camilla gone up to bed, has she?" her father-in-law asked then, coming up to salute her other cheek more warmly than Hunt had done.

"Yes, nearly an hour since, your grace."

"I'll go up and greet her, then," he said with a broad smile for both of them. Nodding placidly, he sauntered out of the room. Whatever was troubling Hunt did not seem to be preying on the duke's mind.

Holly turned nervously back to her husband, wondering how she could ask about what was going on without sounding too eager or interested.

"We have been expecting your return a week and more," he said before she could speak.

"Yes, well, the duchess put off our departure until the coach could be resprung. Not that it made for a faster journey, mind you!"

She was gratified by a faint spark of answering humour in Hunt's eyes. "And you were trapped in the coach with her the whole way. Poor Holly." His gaze softened and she felt an instant response.

"Not so poor," she said, taking a step towards him. A muffled cough from the doorway halted her.

Instantly the tenderness was gone as Hunt swung round to face his secretary. "Ah, there you are, Simmons. I require you to take down a letter. You were not already abed, I hope?"

"No, my lord." The man hesitated, glancing at Holly.

"I was just going upstairs." She forced herself to speak brightly to mask the stab of disappointment she felt. "Good night, my lord."

The marquess nodded almost absently. The troubled, shuttered look was back, and she wondered if he had already forgotten she was there. Feeling vaguely bereft, she made her lonely way up the stairs.

Hunt also felt a pang of loss as he watched her go—he had looked forward to her first night back in Town. At Wickburn, they had come close to patching things up, and he had hopes that they might now complete the process. Almost at once, though, his thoughts turned back to the matter at hand.

He was unsure whether his father fully appreciated the gravity of the situation at the Foreign Office, since nothing seemed to ruffle the duke's cheerful calm. Hunt had long faced the fact that his father's intellect was not of the first order. Wickburn's diplomatic skills consisted primarily in his genial affability. Hunt was sure he would have been politely removed from his post years ago had Hunt not worked tirelessly as his aide, covering his father's worst blunders before they could be detected.

Now, though, it appeared more likely than ever that Hunt would be promoted to a position where he could be of little help to his father, if of rather more use to England. But before he could feel comfortable accepting such a post, he was first determined to solve the mystery surrounding an event that ironically made his appointment almost certain.

Leaning against the mantel, Hunt began to dictate yet another unsatisfactory report to Lord Castlereagh.

THE MOOD IN LONDON, Holly soon found, was still fairly jubilant, for Wellington had continued to advance against Napoléon's troops and nearly every week brought news of fresh victories. She hoped that this relaxed atmosphere might make it easier for her to discover what had brought Hunt and the duke to Town last month—and what Teasdale was currently plotting.

"Do you come with us to the ridotto tonight, brother?" she enquired of Reginald two days after their arrival. She had not had a single moment alone with Hunt since that first night, but she rather suspected that Reginald had.

"Aye, Mother insists, especially since it is by no means certain that Father or Hunt will be able to attend, what with this continuing uproar at the Foreign Office. Not that I mind, especially. A ridotto is bound to be vastly more amusing than the usual diplomatic fare—the masses always add a note of piquancy to an event, don't you think?"

Holly ignored the question. "So they still have not settled that business, have they?" she asked casually, trying to give the impression that she knew all about it.

"Not yet. And I wonder now if they ever will. After all, Meecham was the best man they had for organizing this sort of an internal investigation."

"Lord Meecham? Is he not the other man being considered for the post of permanent undersecretary?" That much information, at least, she had been able to glean from Camilla. She picked up a magazine from the table beside her and began to leaf through it.

"Yes, I'd say Hunt has that one in the bag now, with Meecham dead. He seems more concerned with discovering the murderer, though, than securing Castlereagh's final approval. Perhaps he believes the one will lead to the other."

The magazine nearly fell from Holly's suddenly nerveless fingers. "Dead?" she asked shakily. "Lord Meecham was murdered?"

Reginald looked at her strangely. "Thought you knew. It's all over the Foreign Office, though they've done a good job keeping it out of the papers. Seems he had nearly discovered who their traitor was—" He frowned. "You did know about *that,* didn't you?"

She nodded hastily.

"Good. Wouldn't want Hunt to think I can't be trusted with this sort of information. Anyway, Meecham must have been even closer than he realized, for there's little doubt it was the traitor who killed him. It's put a scare into the paid informants, apparently, for Hunt is having a devil of a time getting any of them to open up now." He shook his head. "Never thought I'd see my straitlaced brother involved in something so unsavoury. Not his sort of thing at all, I should think."

Holly said nothing, remembering what Noel had written on that score in his last letter. Perhaps Hunt had been more involved in such matters all along than anyone in the family suspected.

"Well, if Hunt hasn't mentioned any of this to you, pray don't let on I've told you," Reginald cautioned her when she remained silent.

"Of course not," she assured him. "But thank you for telling me, Reg. Hunt has been so preoccupied that I was worried about him. At least now I understand what he is up against." And what she was up against, as well, she added silently.

Holly had thoroughly dissected this information and had determined what her next step had to be by the time Teasdale accosted them at the ridotto in the gardens of Carlton House that night. But even knowing what she did, she found it almost impossible to believe that this polished, seemingly civilized man could actually be a murderer.

"Good to see you again, Reg!" he exclaimed jovially, clapping Reginald on the shoulder. "And you are both looking as lovely as ever, your grace, my lady." He bowed to Camilla and Holly. For the moment, he seemed all affability, his expression holding no threat. "It's a wonder I was able to locate you in this mob." He gestured at the press of humanity around him.

Holly forced a brilliant smile to her lips. "It is fortunate indeed, Mr. Teasdale. I had wondered when we might have the pleasure of your company again, now we are returned to Town." She knew that Reginald and the duchess might wonder at her words, but there was no possibility of privacy in this crowd, and she feared that if she did not face Teasdale at once she would lose her nerve.

"I am flattered, Lady Vandover," he responded. "I have missed your sparkling conversation, as well." She was sure she did not imagine the meaning in his tone. "Perhaps you will be so kind as to honour me with a dance?"

Fighting an instinctive revulsion, she assented. As he led her into the milling throng of dancers, Holly girded herself to say what she must while she had the opportunity.

"It pains me, my lady, to find that your influence over your husband is not so great as I had hoped," said her partner while she was still ordering her thoughts. "'Twould be a shame if he were to go the way of his predecessor in this investigation."

For an instant she was shocked speechless at this blatant admission and threat, but she quickly found her tongue. "You must know, sir, that if aught happened to my husband my silence would no longer be assured. He is your insurance as much as I am his."

He regarded her narrowly while the movement of the dance took them a pace or two apart. When they came back together he hissed, "Surely you do not forget your brother? His safety also rests in your hands."

"Ah, yes, my brother," she replied quickly, before they were forced to move apart again. This was the opening she had hoped for. "I wished to speak to you of him. You have proved yourself capable of exceeding ruthlessness." He bowed slightly, as though she complimented him. "What assurance have I that my brother is safe even now? I have received no letters from him. For aught I know, you had him hanged months ago."

His eyes now glittered dangerously, but she thought she detected a trace of concern in their depths. She allowed him to think over her question during the next few movements of the dance, focusing her attention on her steps.

"You play a dangerous game, my lady," he finally said, his voice low and vicious.

She trilled a high laugh. "La! Surely you will not murder me here, in the Regent's own gardens, sir?" They were the very words she had been repeating to herself to shore up her courage during the exchange.

"We will not always be in so public a setting," he reminded her.

Holly lifted her chin defiantly. "You know less of women than I imagined if you believe a threat against me likely to carry more weight than one against my husband or brother, Mr. Teasdale." She kept her voice and gaze absolutely steady.

The music ended and he offered his arm. With exaggerated graciousness, she took it.

"I will contrive to bring you proof of your brother's safety within the week, my lady," he murmured just before they rejoined Reginald and the duchess. "Whether that safety—or Vandover's—continues, however, is entirely up to you."

With that she had to be satisfied—for the moment.

True to his word, five days after the Regent's ridotto, Holly received an innocuous letter that proved to be a blank sheet folded around a message from Noel. It was dated only three weeks ago. She had no idea whether Teasdale had deciphered their code, but it scarcely mattered, as Noel had written of nothing of importance. Not a word did he say about the recent ugly developments at the Foreign Office, or about Hunt's role in the investigation, as she had rather hoped he might. Neither did he mention his own covert activities.

The whole of the letter, which was much longer than his previous ones, detailed only the unpleasantness of the life he had been leading in France, giving her the impression he had written it more in a spurt of homesickness than through any desire to impart information.

At least he was still safe, she thought belatedly. She read it through again, consideringly. There was nothing in the letter that could be damaging. Pursing her lips, she refolded the letter and tucked it into the drawer of her writing desk. She would save this letter. Perhaps it could be used to prove to her husband—or to the government—that Noel was working for England, in case Teasdale attempted to carry out his threat.

WITH NOEL'S SAFETY assured, at least for the moment, Holly's next task was to somehow persuade her husband to disengage himself from the investigation—though how she was to do that when they scarcely ever spoke to each other she didn't know. Nor did she think it likely that she would be successful, even if the opportunity arose. Still, she would have to try—Hunt's life might depend upon it.

The opportunity she waited for occurred two nights later. For the first time since her return to London, Hunt and the duke remained at home for the evening. By sheer coincidence, the duchess had chosen that same day to be stricken by a headache that necessitated cancelling that night's activities.

During dinner, Hunt and his father discussed the progress of the war, with an occasional comment by Holly and, less frequently, by Reginald. After dinner, the duke went upstairs to sit with Camilla, and Reginald announced his intention of visiting a private art exhibition with a few friends, leaving Holly and Hunt alone in the parlour.

"No doubt you are glad of an evening to relax, my lord," said Holly before the silence in the room could become awkward. "Such a busy schedule as you have been keeping must be fatiguing. You have not been to bed before one o'clock since I returned." She had lain awake most of those nights, listening as he prepared for bed in his own chamber, longing for him to come to hers.

Hunt poured himself a modest measure of brandy and seated himself beside her. "Pray believe me when I say it has not been through my own choice. The Foreign Office has been in rather an uproar of late."

She put a hand on his sleeve. "It is that investigation still, is it not? The one you spoke of last spring?"

He nodded. "Things are far more serious now, I fear. Murder has been done."

Holly did not have to feign the shudder that ran through her. His words reminded her forcibly of what was at stake. "Murder! Does this mean that you are at risk, as well?"

"Perhaps some slight risk," he conceded. "However, I am being more cautious than poor Meecham. Every clue I find, though there have been damned few so far, is put into writing at once, so that the traitor would gain little by my demise. Meecham hoped for a political coup and therefore kept his findings to himself. 'Tis one thing that makes my job so difficult now."

Holly bit her lip. Surely if Teasdale knew that everything was down in writing, Hunt's life must be safe? But she dared not risk that. "Please, Hunt," she said with sudden urgency, "leave this investigation to others! I...could not bear to see you hurt."

He frowned down at her. "What is this? Last spring you begged me to allow you to help in this investigation, and now you warn me away from it? I thank you for your concern, of course, but is it not a bit out of character?"

She knew that he referred not only to what she had said last spring, but also to her coldness to him over the summer. "I—I did not realize then what risks were involved." That was true enough! "I would not wish to help now, of course."

"That is as well, for I would not allow it. But this is something that I must do, Holly, for reasons both political and personal. Meecham was a friend."

For a moment she said nothing, acutely conscious that she would do the very same in his place. Her respect for her husband, and her love for him, had never been greater. More than ever she longed to tell him the whole, about Teasdale, Noel and her own stupidity last spring. But fear for his safety and for his career, which meant so much to him, prevented her—and spurred her to try again.

"I understand, Hunt, but still I wish you would not." When there was no softening in his expression, she asked impulsively, "Can you at least tell me how the investigation is going? Have you a list of likely suspects?" Perhaps if she could convince Teasdale that he was in no immediate danger of exposure—

"I'm sorry, Holly." Hunt's voice was cool, a hint of the suspicion she had feared in his eyes. "If you recall, it was your preference that we not exchange confidences. Nor would it be appropriate in this circumstance."

She stared at him helplessly, realizing that he was right. She could scarcely expect him to be forthcoming with sensitive information after her own secretiveness. And now he had withdrawn from her again.

"Promise me you will take care, Hunt," she said finally, reaching out tentatively in hopes of bridging the gulf she had created.

"Of course." He rose before she could touch him. "If you will excuse me, madam, I have some paperwork to attend to."

Again, he did not come to her that night. Staring sleeplessly up at the canopy above her, Holly wished she had never brought up the subject of the wretched investigation. She had accomplished nothing, and lost an opportunity to sleep in Hunt's arms once more.

"WHY IS IT all the truly breathtaking ladies are married?" asked Sir Gregory Thurston with a dramatic sigh, as he led Holly from the floor of Lord and Lady Bellerby's imposing ballroom a few evenings later. "My heart is like to break at your unapproachable loveliness."

Holly chuckled and rapped his knuckles with her fan, as she had seen other ladies do. She had set herself to learn the art of light flirtation, thinking it might be useful both with her husband and in her dealings with Teasdale. She felt her repartee at the ridotto had been woefully inadequate. "Unapproachable? Did I not just grant you a dance, sir?"

"Ah, what is a dance, but a tantalizing moment in your company? It only reminds me of what I am missing when you are not by my side." He gazed soulfully at her and Holly laughed again.

She had seen him put on this same performance with at least three other ladies, all married, and knew it was but a game.

"La, sir, but you will turn my head with such talk," she said playfully. If nothing else, such harmless flirting served to distract her from her problems—and her loneliness.

From across the room, Hunt watched as his wife laughed up into the face of a man well known for his pursuit of married ladies. He had been kept late at an extended meeting with two of the undercover agents carrying out his investigation. Perhaps he should have made an effort to get here earlier.

Not since the early days of their marriage had he seen Holly looking so carefree, so...happy. It would seem that spending so much time apart had the opposite effect on her that it had on him. He began to make his way around the edge of the ballroom towards her.

When the crowd shifted a moment later, he found himself face to face with a still-laughing Holly. "Good evening, my lady," he said with a stiff bow.

"Hunt! You managed to come." She snatched her hand from Sir Gregory's sleeve and turned quickly towards him.

Reading dismay into her expression of surprise, Hunt clenched his jaw and flicked a glance at Sir Gregory, who bowed respectfully before melting into the surrounding throng. "I can see you did not expect me, though I told you I would try to attend."

"You said the same about the Herveys' card party last night," she reminded him. "Should I have waited at home on the chance that you would return to escort me?"

"'Twould have been a better choice than simpering after a fellow like Thurston," he snapped, jealousy and anger suddenly overcoming his judgement. "It appears that you require closer supervision than Camilla can provide." He had tried so hard, all these months, to convince himself that there was no one else, but now—

Now Holly was angry, as well, her eyes glittering ominously. "I do not require anyone's *supervision,* my lord," she almost spat at him.

People were beginning to glance their way, Hunt realized belatedly. He gripped her arm. "Come, madam, I believe this dance is mine." Without another word, he swung her out onto the floor for the country dance just forming.

Holly seethed all through that silent dance. She had done nothing wrong. Not this time. In fact, everything she *had* done, all the fear, the pain she had endured, was for Hunt's sake. And this was how he repaid her—with petty jealousy over a nobody like Sir Gregory, whom she had scarcely met before tonight. It was so unfair.

She was not in a mood to be reasonable or to see things from Hunt's perspective. Instead, she felt that he should somehow understand what she was going through and offer to take the burden from her shoulders.

The rest of the evening passed in chilly silence. Hunt danced with her only once more, but never left her side, effectively discouraging anyone else from partnering her.

Holly would not have minded so much—might, in fact, have felt flattered at his jealousy—had he been the least bit attentive. Instead, he ignored her.

In fact, Hunt was not as unaware of Holly as she imagined. Even when he was not looking at her, she tantalized him—her voice, her body, even her scent called out to him. He wanted her desperately, but all he had managed to do was act like a jealous fool, making wild accusations that had no basis in fact.

The pressure he had been under lately must surely be to blame. That very afternoon, young Teasdale had had the effrontery to hint openly that Hunt himself might be the leak, citing his French wife as evidence. Hunt had brought him down hard for the suggestion, but it rankled. And now, in spite of himself, every insinuation Camilla had ever made about Holly's nationality came flooding back to haunt him. None of it was true, of course, but—

"Make your curtsies to our hosts, madam," he said abruptly. "It is time we took our leave." He needed to get out of the crowd, to think.

HOLLY THOUGHTFULLY CHEWED the end of her pen before writing the final coded sentence of her letter to Noel. She had little hope that it would reach him, but she had to try just once more. After all, Teasdale could not have her watched every minute. And if she and Noel worked together, they might be able to bring him to justice in time to save her marriage.

In the carriage last night, Holly had finally swallowed her pride and told Hunt she was sorry she had spoken so sharply. He had looked at her strangely—looked at her for quite a long time, in fact—before telling her not to mention it. She had thought that things would be better after that, but upon reaching Wickburn House he had let her off and directed the coachman to drive on rather than accompanying her up to bed, as she had hoped he might.

She had slept little, her mind twisting this way and that, seeking a way out of the trap she was in. Only one thing was clear—she could no longer handle it alone. But she had already alienated her husband, perhaps beyond repair. Her only other hope was Noel.

Holly folded and sealed the letter with wax, though not her seal, then glanced at the window. It was still early. Not even the servants would be awake as yet. She pulled on a simple gown that buttoned up the front and then a dark cloak. Silently opening her chamber door, she peered up and down the hallway to be certain it was empty. It was.

Her thin slippers made no sound on the carpet as she hurried to the servants' staircase. Below, all was quiet, as well, and she made her way to the kitchen door and out into the alleyway at the rear of the house. Turning to the left, she hurried along to the mews that served this and two other streets. A few stable-boys were stirring, but she doubted that any would recognize her. Still, to be on the safe side, she pulled the hood of her cloak close about her face, completely concealing her ebony hair.

It was only a matter of half a mile to the Grey Goose Inn, and she covered it in under ten minutes. Hurrying round to the stables, she was relieved to find Peter already there.

He glanced up in surprise when she said his name, his quick smile fading to a troubled frown. "Ye shouldn't ought to be here, m' lady," he whispered, looking around nervously.

She spoke hurriedly, without preamble. "I know that Teasdale paid you, and probably threatened you, so that you would not deliver my last letter. I do not blame you, for he has frightened me, as well. But it is of vital importance that this letter *does* reach France." She pulled out the letter, and a guinea. "I don't like to ask you to take such a risk, but might this be ample compensation?"

His eyes widened at the sight of the golden coin. "Aye, m' lady," he breathed almost reverently. "I'd near swim the channel meself for that much."

"Oh, thank you, Peter, thank you! Now, not a word to anyone that I was here!"

"Mum's the word, m' lady," he murmured, pocketing both the letter and the money.

For an instant, Holly felt a pang of conscience. Peter was young to be working for his living, much less taking the kind of risk she requested. He was thin, too. She sighed. There was really no other way—and there were dozens, even hundreds, of boys in far worse straits about the city. If all went well, perhaps she could come back and hire him for a post at Wickburn House.

Holly's heart was lighter during the walk back. Her letter was on its way, or so she had reason to hope. Once Hunt received that appointment, as he surely would, she would be able to tell him the truth and finally be out from under the terrible burden she'd borne for so long. Secure in that lofty position, no doubt he could have Teasdale arrested at once and their lives could resume the course they had begun last Christmas.

Occupied in such happy thoughts, she soon reached the back door of Wickburn House. One of the maids was drawing water in the kitchen when she peeped in, but no one else seemed to be about. She waited until the girl went into the scullery, then slipped through the kitchens and up the back stairs.

She paused in the shadows at the end of the hall to be certain that no one on the second floor was yet awake, then as silently as before, she crept to her chamber door. Her hand was on the handle when the door flew open with a crash. She gasped and shrank back, her heart in her throat.

Hunt stood there, his eyes glittering with suppressed emotion as he demanded through clenched teeth, "And just where have *you* been all night, madam wife?"

CHAPTER TEN

HOLLY HAD ALREADY begun glibly repeating the excuse she had prepared about taking the air when the full impact of her husband's accusation hit her. "All night?" she interrupted herself incredulously.

Hunt's eyes narrowed dangerously. "Don't try to play the innocent with me—not now. Nearly half an hour since I went into your bedroom to find you gone. You did *not* 'step out for a breath of air.' It appears my original suspicions were well founded. Perhaps Camilla had the right of it with her hints about Frenchwomen's morals!"

Stung by the injustice of his accusation, Holly did not pause to wonder why he had come to her room in the first place. Nor did she hear the pain beneath the anger in his voice. "So, I am to be tried and convicted solely on the basis of my blood?" She put every scrap of scorn she could summon into her tone. "In that case, I see no point in attempting to deny it!"

"It would do you no good if you did." Hunt's voice struck her like a lash but she refused to cringe. "I had assumed you held a proper appreciation for the dignity due the name you now bear. It seems I was wrong. But you will not cuckold me again if I have to keep you under lock and key to prevent it."

Another door opened farther down the hall and Hunt grasped her painfully by the arm, pulling her into her sitting-room and slamming the door behind him. "This will remain our secret, madam. I would not have word get back to my grandmother of your perfidy, nor be made a laughingstock about Town."

Holly was angrier than she had ever been in her life. How *dared* he? And after all she had endured for his sake! "You'd best lock me up in truth then, my lord, for surely you cannot trust me to do anything that is right or honourable." Her words dripped with sarcasm, but he seemed to take them at face value.

"I'll go you one better than that. Your mother wrote you last week suggesting that you visit her, did she not? You will do so. I will arrange for your departure within the week."

"You intend to send me back to my mother like an erring child? I won't go." Though she almost feared to stay here with Hunt in this mood, Holly had not the least desire to be sent home in disgrace. How Blanche would gloat!

"You have little choice. When you made your vows to me you gave me complete control over your person. I intend to exert it." A smile devoid of humour twisted his face.

Holly felt chilled and humiliated, realizing that he was absolutely correct. There was nothing she could do to prevent him from sending her away. Gathering the tattered shreds of her pride about her, she raised her chin. "I go to my mother's, then. But I will go in the crested carriage and bring my personal servants with me." That would help to cow Blanche, at least.

"Of course," he said coldly. "We would not wish the world to suspect the reason for your departure. You will merely visit your mother for a while." He swept her a bow which was a masterpiece of mockery and left her.

The moment the door closed behind him, Holly sank down onto the nearest chair, afraid that her legs would not support her any longer. Though she was still stubbornly determined not to deny such an outrageous accusation, based on nothing more than a half-hour's absence from her chamber, her husband's lack of trust hurt her deeply.

"Oh, Noel," she whispered aloud to the silent room, "I should have waited for your return, after all. I fear this marriage was the greatest mistake of my life!"

THE COOLNESS that had existed between the marquess and his wife last summer was as nothing to the estrangement between them now. It appeared to Holly that her husband could scarcely bear to look at her. Nor did she feel much more kindly disposed towards him.

Still, as she watched his profile from across a crowded room during Lady Stilton's musicale, her heart contracted. He had meant so much to her—he had been almost her whole world. Mere words, however harsh, could not change that.

The duchess seemed delighted at Holly's sudden "decision" to visit her mother. "If she said she was ailing in her last letter, of course you must go to her," she said. "Daughters can be a great comfort at such times, or so I have been told. And you may well find that her illness is more serious than she has led you to believe. Mothers do tend to spare their children worry, you know."

Maman's ailment was purely fictitious, invented by Hunt to account for Holly's visit, but of course she could not say so. Not for the world would she have the duchess guess the true state of things, though how anyone could miss the strain between Hunt and herself she didn't know.

"Yes, it is undoubtedly best that I go to see her. It seems unfair for my sister to bear all the burden of her care." The thought of Blanche bearing any burdens was slightly ludicrous, but she found no difficulty in keeping her expression sober.

During the remaining days before her departure, Holly noticed that Hunt managed to attend every evening function that she did, even if he never spoke to her. Even during the day, he saw to it that she was never left on her own; if the function she attended was not solely for ladies, Reginald contrived to accompany her. The duchess alone was no longer considered a suitable chaperon, it appeared.

On the afternoon before she was to leave, Holly asked Reginald to take her to the Royal Academy in Somerset House. Normally, he spent the majority of his time there, and she felt badly that he had neglected his artistic pursuits this week because of her quarrel with Hunt. It was not his fault, after all.

He seemed delighted at the chance to show her the rooms he habitually haunted, introducing her to a few of his fellow artists who happened to be there.

"Nothing of mine is displayed here as yet, but it is only a matter of time," he informed her confidently as they traversed the enormous, echoing exhibition hall.

Apart from the students and instructors, the Academy rooms were largely deserted. When Holly remarked on it, more to divert her thoughts than because she was actually curious, he explained that only a select few were allowed in when a regular exhibition was not going on.

"You are very lucky to be seeing it at all, I can tell you, sister. Rank alone will not gain one admittance. Only merit."

Holly murmured something polite, her mind elsewhere.

Reginald paused in his stately walk to look seriously down at her. "I can see your heart is not in this today. You are not leaving Town because of your mother's health, are you? Would you like to tell me about it? It will go no further, I assure you."

Looking up, Holly saw that his blue eyes, so like Hunt's and their father's, were kind. Though she smiled her thanks at his concern and shook her head, her face warmed with embarrassment. She could scarcely tell him that Hunt was sending her home like a child in disgrace. "I fear I cannot. It . . . it is a private matter."

Reginald looked as though he meant to pursue the matter, but then, glancing past her, his expression changed.

"Ah, Teasdale! Come to improve your skill with the oils, have you?"

Holly nearly whirled around, barely catching herself in time to turn in a more dignified manner. She had not spoken with Teasdale since receiving Noel's letter. She had almost begun to hope he had left Town. He regarded her mockingly, she thought, though his words were directed at Reginald.

"Nay, I merely came to find a quiet place to think," he replied. "Indeed, I do so little here that I am surprised one of the masters has not revoked your standing invitation to me. But why are you not attending a class?" His glance strayed back to Holly.

"Just showing m' sister-in-law about my second home." Reginald waved his arm expansively. "She goes into the country to visit her mother tomorrow, you know."

"No, I didn't know." Teasdale's eyes seemed to bore into her. "London will be bereft at your absence, my lady."

"Come, Mr. Teasdale," she said impulsively, "surely you, too, must have some favourites among the works displayed here. Will you not point them out to me?" Perhaps if she could be private with Teasdale for a moment, she could discover whether he had intercepted her letter to Noel—and what he meant to do in her absence. Angry as she was with Hunt, she did not want to see him harmed.

He picked up on her cue at once. "I do, but I fear that Reg will make disparaging comments upon my taste if I reveal them in his presence. If I could show them to you alone, without risking his judgement . . . ?"

"Certainly, certainly," agreed Reginald affably. "I need to speak with old Hoarwell for a moment, anyway." He sauntered through one of the tall doorways.

"You had something you wished to tell me?" Teasdale asked sharply, throwing Holly somewhat off her guard. But suddenly she felt a surge of relief. If he knew she had written to her brother again, he would have something to say about it, some threat to make.

"Yes," she improvised quickly so as not to arouse his suspicions. "As Reginald said, I leave Town tomorrow, and I wanted your assurance that my husband will be safe. Derbyshire is but a day's drive from London, should I find it necessary to return."

The very amiability of his smile made her stiffen, but he only said, "Not to worry, my lady. I have decided that Lord Vandover's demise, however accidental it might appear, would increase the risks to myself. No, his *life* is in no danger, despite his continued involvement in the investigation. There, have I set your mind at rest?"

Holly regarded him doubtfully, trying to decipher his words and tone. Plainly he meant more than he was saying. But already Reginald was returning. "Perfectly, sir, I thank you. And it may surprise you to hear that your tastes are not so very different from my brother-in-law's," she concluded more loudly.

Teasdale bowed and then left them, and Lord Reginald turned back to the paintings, pointing out the more notable specimens. Holly pretended to listen, grateful that he did not seek to reintroduce the topic of her troubles with Hunt.

That evening Holly pleaded the headache to avoid accompanying the others to Lady Castlereagh's card party. Her absence would be remarked, she knew, but she felt unequal to the task of smiling for hours, pretending that all was well. She retired to her room directly after dinner, intending to dissect Teasdale's words and her situation one more time, even though such a course would likely make her fictitious headache a reality.

Mabel had already completed the packing for tomorrow's journey, for they were to leave at first light. Holly allowed her abigail to prepare her for bed, sitting passively at the dressing-table while her hair was brushed out.

Even after Mabel had left her, Holly continued to stare into the glass, remembering. Hunt had cared for her once, she was certain. He had never said that he loved her in so many words, but he had shown his affection clearly both before and after their marriage. And she had fallen quite hopelessly in love with him.

But now, with her silence and secrets, she feared that she had finally killed whatever affection he had held for her. And if that were so, what sort of life awaited her? One of utter loneliness. If he chose, he could leave her at her mother's house indefinitely while he pursued his own life—and his own pleasures—in Town.

He could even take a mistress.

A surge of jealousy, the first she could ever remember feeling, swept through her at the thought of another woman enjoying those intimacies with her husband that had been so special to her. And hard on the heels of that jealousy came an intense longing. Only once in the past half year had Hunt come to her bed. Though pride might make her deny her love, her body most assuredly missed him.

Almost as though she had summoned him with her thoughts, the door to her dressing-room opened and Hunt stepped into the chamber, clad in the midnight blue silk dressing-gown she remembered so well.

"I thought it best to take my leave of you tonight," he said with cold formality. "Thus we can avoid what the others might expect to be a touching scene in the morning." His eyes were as dark as the silk he wore.

Though his tone chilled her, Holly scarcely heeded his words. She was striving to subdue the clamour her body set up at the sight of him. She must *not* let him see how he still affected her. It would be too humiliating.

Hunt wasn't sure what had prompted him to come. He had intended to remain completely aloof from his wife until her departure, for fear that his anger—perfectly righteous anger—might not hold up against her nearness. At

Lady Stilton's two nights ago he had nearly given in. Holly had looked so lovely, with her hair in ebony ringlets, the deep peach silk of her gown making her skin and eyes glow, that he had been ready to forgive her almost anything to have her in his arms again. He had resisted only by refusing to look in her direction for the greater part of the evening.

But how was he to resist her now? She had risen at his entrance and stood before him, a breathtaking vision, her hair flowing unbound past her shoulders, her body calling to him through the almost transparent white peignoir she wore. He should not have come.

"Yes, they might well look for tenderness, even tears, as we will be parting for...months." There was a soft question in her voice. "A private goodbye will circumvent such expectations. Very foresighted of you, my lord."

Hunt felt that he had never been less foresighted in his life not to realize what an effect she would have on him. "Perhaps it need not be so long," he said tentatively, vainly trying to reassemble the anger he knew he should feel at her betrayal. How many months had passed since he had bedded her? Far too many. God, he wanted her!

"Perhaps not," agreed Holly, swaying slightly forward, though she did not actually take a step.

For the barest instant, Hunt hesitated. He knew once he touched her he would be lost. But his body spoke louder than his reason, and without conscious intent his feet moved forward until she was only inches away. He could smell the faint perfume of her hair, feel the radiant warmth of her skin against his throat.

"My lord?" It was almost a sigh, and it undid him completely.

His hands came up from his sides of their own volition and tangled themselves in her hair. He tipped her face up and hungrily sought her lips with his. She responded with equal hunger, drawing his tongue deeply into her mouth, entwining it with her own. Hunt heard a deep groan and realized it had come from his throat. He wrapped his arms around her, never breaking the kiss, pulling her tighter and tighter against him, his body a raging torrent.

Holly's hands slid between them, and then beneath his dressing-gown to caress his back. Wildly, almost frantically, Hunt tugged at the ribbons securing her peignoir, breaking them when they did not give way at once. With a convulsive motion, he shrugged out of his dressing-gown, revelling in the feel of his unclothed length against hers.

Still Holly did not draw back. Instead she rubbed against him, her bare breasts against his chest igniting even hotter fires within him. He swept her up and bore her to the bed, joining her atop the quilts. Feeling he was about to explode, he entered her almost at once. She was wet and ready to receive him. They writhed together for a brief few moments, then gasped simultaneously at the blessed release.

Though his heartbeat gradually slowed, Hunt found he had no desire to return to reason—not yet. She felt so good, so right, in his arms. After a few minutes' rest, he began to move within her again, this time more slowly.

Holly felt a thrill of surprise. Braced as she was for his withdrawal once his passion was spent, Hunt's renewed caresses sent a wave of pleasure through her that went far beyond the physical sensations they aroused. That first coupling was all too easy to explain. Denied cravings had needed an outlet, for them both. She had been startled, but not really shocked at the violence of their joining.

But he was not leaving. Not yet. It must mean... His hand slid between them and she abruptly lost the desire, even the ability, to reason as she again gave herself up to passion.

NOT UNTIL Mabel's tap came at the door did Hunt leave her. They had made love twice more, finally falling into a deep sleep, bodies still entwined. At the maid's gentle knock, they both roused.

Holly looked up at the shadow that was Hunt's face above her and felt herself blushing. She was glad it was not yet light enough for him to see her clearly. What could she say? What would he say? They had spoken scarcely a word to each other during their long, passionate night together.

"You'd best get ready to go," he said huskily after a lengthy pause.

She nodded, unable to speak for the sudden pain that knifed through her. He still wanted her to leave.

"Much needs to be said between us," he said, then, "but now is not the time."

A tendril of hope curled through her. "Soon, though?" she managed to ask.

"I will be leaving for the Shires in two or three weeks for the hunting season. Perhaps by Christmas..." His voice trailed off, but she could hear the question in it.

"By Christmas," she replied, more firmly than she felt.

He kissed her once more, hard, and then left her, disappearing so quickly through the dressing-room door that she almost wondered whether she had dreamed the whole night. But no, the bedclothes were scattered about, half of them on the floor, and her peignoir lay by her dressing-table, its ribbons broken. Hurriedly, she bundled the blankets back onto the bed and pulled the torn garment about her before calling out to Mabel that she could enter.

HOLLY'S HOMECOMING was not all that she could have wished, though it gave her a spurt of satisfaction to see Blanche's face when she strode regally into the house, four servants in tow. She had dressed in her finest travelling gown and cloak for the occasion and had Mabel take especial pains with her hair, retouching it at the last stop. She knew she looked every inch the Marchioness of Vandover, and Blanche's jealous expression confirmed it.

This time she intended to set the tone of her visit at the outset, making it clear that she was no longer at her older sister's beck and call. Looking at Blanche's peevish, puffy face as she delivered a sour welcome, Holly wondered how she had ever held her sister in awe.

Since she had sent word ahead that she was coming, her sister had waited a late supper for her. "Maman is already abed," Blanche told her as they took their seats. "I did not wish her to tire herself with fussing about tonight so I allowed her to believe you were to arrive tomorrow. 'Twould have made more sense, you realize, for you to stop at an inn and arrive here in the morning."

Holly refused to apologize, even with her expression. "I look forward to seeing her then. You and she have been keeping well, I hope?"

"Maman is unequal to handling the estate on her own, nor have I the strength to manage it all." Blanche assumed a martyred expression. "I have written to Upper Canada to tell Noel, but no doubt he is too busy to come. His most recent letter sounded as if he had not even read the one Maman sent him last month."

The versatile Mary bustled in just then, serving soup and cold tongue. Holly waited until she had gone before speaking again, something she never would have thought to do before the dowager's training.

"Maman's letter may very well have been missent. I hear it happens often in wartime."

Blanche sniffed, but after a few moments of silence she spoke again. "Have you met very many officers in London, then? A regiment was quartered here for a few weeks last summer, as Maman may have written you."

Holly hid a smile. Her mother's letter had also mentioned Blanche's hopes of attaching one of the officers, she recalled. A circumstance which had plainly not come to pass. "A few," she admitted, and proceeded to share some amusing stories of Town from last spring and summer.

Blanche contrived to appear disinterested, though her heightened complexion and occasional swift glances told

Holly that she was listening closely. For the first time in her life, Holly felt a little bit sorry for Blanche. She realized that despite her problems, her own life was far richer than her sister's.

The next morning, even before Holly had dressed, her mother came to her room. "Mary tells me that you arrived last night, after all. Why did you not wake me?" she demanded, kissing her daughter effusively. "My! But it is good to have you home again."

"'Tis good to see you, too, Maman," said Holly, returning the embrace. "Blanche tells me that the two of you have trouble keeping up with the demands of the estate. Perhaps while I am here I may be of some help to you."

Mrs. Paxton sighed gustily. "I fear I have no head for business or accounts, it is true. And though she insists she can manage things, poor Blanche is so delicate...."

Holly coughed politely. It had always rather amused her—and Noel, too, she remembered—when Blanche had used that excuse to avoid chores. She was still at it, apparently, her innate laziness warring with her penchant for control. "Of course, Maman. I will see what needs to be done."

Though Blanche scoffed and found fault, Holly spent the greater part of the next few days going over the household accounts and consulting with the steward. There was no lack of funds, she found, simply a lack of efficient management. Putting her lessons with the dowager duchess to good use, she began to make some sorely needed changes.

While it gratified her to see the difference her efforts made, that was not the main reason for Holly's industry. As long as she kept busy with such things, she had little time for thought—or despondency.

During the first part of her fourteen-hour drive from London, she had been buoyed by hope after the passionate goodbye she and Hunt had shared. But then, as hour followed dreary hour and she left him farther and farther behind, her spirits drooped. She recalled instead the angry words they had exchanged a week ago.

She feared no amount of passion could erase those memories from her mind—or his. At best, it merely covered the wounds with a thin bandage, hiding them. Still, she was more hopeful than she had been the day before she left London. Hunt had almost promised they would see each other before Christmas. And every day brought more and more good news from abroad; the French had been crushed near Leipzig, and it was rumoured that Paris would fall soon. Surely, by Christmas all need for secrecy would be past.

She was reflecting happily on such thoughts during a brief rest from a morning of preparing baskets for the needy. As she sat in the parlour waiting for Mary to bring in the tea tray, Blanche came in, just returned from a shopping expedition in the village.

"I brought the morning post," she announced loftily. "Here is one for you, *Lady Vandover*, from London." She handed Holly the letter, then pointedly turned her attention to the others she held.

Holly grimaced. Blanche seemed to get a perverse pleasure in calling her by her title and she had given up telling her to stop. Shrugging, she turned her attention to her letter. It was addressed not in Hunt's hand, as she had hoped, but in his mother's. Disappointedly she broke the seal, but after reading only the first few lines she gasped and dropped the letter into her lap.

"What is it?" Blanche could not disguise her curiosity. "You've gone quite white, I declare. Is it bad news?"

"Hunt has been arrested." Feeling as though she had been punched in the stomach, Holly struggled to breathe normally. "He is accused ... of treason!"

CHAPTER ELEVEN

HOLLY ROSE QUICKLY. "I must return to London at once! Blanche, ring for Mary, do."

"Had you not better read the entire letter first?" suggested her sister practically, gesturing at the sheets that had fallen to the floor, her expression almost sympathetic. "Perhaps things are not so bad as they sound."

Holly stopped halfway to the parlour door. "Oh! Yes, I—I suppose so." Though her every instinct screamed at her to hurry, she forced herself to concentrate as she perused the remainder of the lengthy missive.

Hunt had been seized outside Wickburn House two nights since and searched. The duchess did not know the details of what had happened, as she had been away from home at the time, but she and the duke were informed that the marquess was being held on suspicion of passing classified information to the French.

> It is Hunt's wish, that you remain in Derbyshire for the present. In fact, he is most adamant on that point. No doubt he is right, for you would not wish to be involved in the inevitable scandal attending his arrest. But pray be easy—Wickburn is conducting a full investigation, and will never allow his heir to be executed for what must surely be a false accusation.
>
> Fondly, etc., Camilla Wickburn

Holly sank back into the chair she had quitted so violently a moment ago. "Hunt...Hunt wishes me to stay here," she said woodenly. "The duchess speaks of scandal, but I care nothing for that." Suddenly she rose again, crushing the letter between her fists. "No, I must go! I must discover—" Decisively, she rang the bell herself.

Blanche stared, quite obviously at a loss. "But Lord Vandover said you were to stay here," she protested weakly. "Surely you will not disobey him—and the *duchess?*"

Holly set her mouth into a firm line, her eyes now quite dry. "I must, if ever I expect to become a duchess myself. Ah, Mary, here you are! Pray send word to the stables that my coach is to be made ready, and then go up and help Mabel to pack my things. I intend to leave for London within the hour."

"HAVE YOU NOTHING to say in your defence?" the frustrated barrister demanded, raking one hand through his mousy hair. One of the best King's Counsels in England, the man was being well paid by the Duke of Wickburn to defend his son from the outrageous charges against him. But his client was making his job extremely difficult.

"Only that I am no traitor," replied Hunt stubbornly.

"Then why will you not tell me how that letter came to be found on your person? You do not even deny writing it yourself."

Hunt said nothing. Though a few simple words would clear him, those same words could conceivably send his wife to the gallows.

On the day of his arrest, he had received an anonymous note saying that Lady Vandover had been seen accepting a letter from a known French agent the week before. Hunt had not believed it, of course, but with the investigation going so poorly, he could not afford to overlook any clue that might lead to the traitor. He had gone home at once to search Holly's chamber.

When he discovered the coded letter, Hunt's first feeling, incredibly, was one of relief. Holly hadn't been betraying him with another man. The morning he had caught her returning to the house so stealthily, she must have been meeting the French agent mentioned in the note. And it had probably been another such letter that he had caught her burning last May.

But hard on the heels of relief came fear. Treason, after all, was a capital offence. Holly was half-French. For all he knew, she had family or friends who supported Napoléon. He remembered, too, the time she had attempted to talk him out of pursuing the investigation. Putting the letter in his pocket, he left Wickburn House to take a walk and think things through. Before he had gone half a block, however, he had been arrested and searched. The letter had been found.

Since then he had said almost nothing. Traitor or no, he would not send Holly to the gallows if his silence could prevent it. He himself was in no real danger, he was certain, even though his refusal to defend himself might lengthen his stay in prison and blast his chances for advancement in the Foreign Office.

He had to admit, though, that the evidence against him was hardly trifling. The experts had not yet been able to completely break the code used in the letter they had found, but they were confident that they soon would. And his position in the Foreign Office made him a perfectly reasonable suspect, particularly since he might be considered to have benefited by Lord Meecham's death....

His defence counselor let out a gusty sigh. "Lord Vandover, you cannot expect me to have the charges against you dismissed if you are unwilling to cooperate. It looks exceedingly bad, you must understand."

Hunt merely shrugged, and the man rose from his place across the narrow table in the centre of the marquess's quarters—the most luxurious available in the King's Bench, though still depressingly Spartan.

"I shall leave you, then. Pray reconsider, my lord, when I return this afternoon."

His face an impassive mask, Hunt watched him go. Scarcely two minutes passed before his father entered.

"Northrup informs me you are being most recalcitrant, my boy!" exclaimed the duke. He glanced around the little chamber and apparently decided against seating himself. "Why will you not tell him what he needs to know?"

Hunt ignored the question, instead enquiring, "Has Camilla yet received a response from my wife?"

Forgetting his earlier reservations, the duke sat heavily in the chair the barrister had just quitted, a worried frown on his broad brow. "Not yet. It must have been quite a shock for her, my lad. Give her time."

Hunt stared past his father at the bars on the windows, a constant reminder that this was not the inn room it otherwise appeared to be. Had Holly's apparent affection for him been false, as well? He didn't want to believe it, but if she would not even write... It appeared his wife was more of a stranger to him than he had thought.

"Yes. Of course," he said bleakly as another piece of his heart died within him.

"WHAT DO YOU MEAN, I cannot go to see him?" After travelling all night in order to reach London early in the day, Holly had already been frustrated in the extreme to wait idly at Wickburn House until one of the family returned. Now she vented that frustration on the duchess. "Of course I must see him—he is my husband!"

"Now, my dear, pray do not take on so." Camilla's soothing tone had quite the opposite effect, making Holly bristle with impatience. "Even I have not been allowed to visit at the prison. Ladies don't, you know."

"Is that a law?" Holly demanded.

"Well...not in the *legal* sense, I suppose, for some of the lower orders imprisoned there do have their wives in to visit. But 'twould be most scandalous. Hunt would never forgive you—or me, either, I daresay. He's been extremely, ah, moody since his arrest, Wickburn tells me."

Holly considered that quite understandable. But plainly she would get no further with her mother-in-law, whose concern for the proprieties was as firmly entrenched as Hunt's. "Is Reginald expected home soon?" she asked the duchess, as calmly as she could.

"Oh! He is at the Academy, as always. Shall I send a message round to him?" Camilla was all affability, now that Holly seemed to have conceded her point.

"Yes, thank you. I should like to speak to him. He *has* seen Hunt, I take it?"

"Nearly every day." The duchess nodded, smiling. "I'll send a footman at once."

Less than half an hour later, Reginald burst into the parlour where Holly waited, relief evident on his face. Holly scarcely noticed his expression, for just behind him Mr. Teasdale strolled into the room.

"You *are* here!" Reginald exclaimed. "I told Hunt you would come, but he didn't believe me."

Holly's attention swung back to her brother-in-law. "Do you mean he sent for me? Your mother said he did not wish me to come to London."

Reginald looked uncomfortable. "Oh, well . . . he didn't *send* for you, precisely. And that is what he *says*. But I think he must secretly have been hoping you would. Stands to reason, after all. You're his wife."

Holly had to smile at Reginald's straightforward naïvety. Plainly he had no inkling of how deep the rift between her and Hunt had become. On that thought, she glanced back to Teasdale, now seated a short distance from her. Though she'd been surprised to see him, it was as well he had come—it saved her hunting him down.

Reginald followed her glance. "Teasdale happened to be at the Academy when the messenger came, and offered to be of assistance," he explained. Teasdale nodded calmly. "He's been a great support to Mother—and to me—during this horrible affair. Why, I can scarcely paint for thinking over what could... That is to say..." He stopped, apparently realizing that his words were scarcely comforting.

"Reg, dear," Holly said quickly, "would you be a dear and run to tell Cook to send up a tea tray? I know it's not the time for it, but I feel a need for something sustaining."

He fairly shot from his chair. "Certainly, certainly. Could use a bit of something myself, now you come to mention it. I'll see to it personally."

The moment he was gone, Holly addressed Teasdale without preamble, her voice low but fierce. "You said that my husband was in no danger, sir. If you adhere so poorly to your bargains, surely you do not expect me to honour mine. You cannot have thought I would remain silent, protecting you, while Hunt goes to the gallows."

To her amazement, Teasdale smiled. "My dear madam, your husband is in no danger, no danger at all—so long as you *do* remain silent."

"No danger?" She was incredulous. "How can you say so? He stands accused of treason!"

"The evidence against him is trifling. With that alone, a conviction is virtually impossible."

"So it is as I thought—you are responsible for his arrest. And what is this 'trifling' evidence? If 'twas enough to get him arrested..."

He shook his head. "I merely whispered into a few ears. A rumour is a powerful thing in wartime, you must realize. I needed Vandover out of the way for a few weeks so that I could make my own, ah, arrangements without interference. But as for the nature of the evidence, why, you provided it yourself, my lady."

"I?" she gasped.

"You do recall the letter from your brother you insisted I give you. I rather feared you might have taken it with you when you left London, but 'twas all I could think of in a pinch. Vandover was getting closer than even he realized with his investigation. Luckily for him—and for you—you left the letter behind so that he was able to find it."

"Noel's letter?" Holly felt more confused than enlightened. She had forgotten all about that letter, and tried now to recall what it had said. "There was nothing in that letter to imply any sort of treasonous activities on the part of Hunt or my brother. I'd have burned it else."

"Precisely why your husband stands in no real danger, my lady. That letter alone cannot convict him. However, there is certain other evidence I could make available to the authorities that would—if I were moved to do so."

"What other evidence? Hunt has done nothing and well you know it!"

His smile became even nastier. "For a price, some people can be persuaded to say—or write—almost anything. As I said, during wartime it takes little to arouse fear. And certain Foreign Office officials are by now exceedingly anxious to find a scapegoat."

Holly blanched. She had no doubt that was true—or that Teasdale would carry out his vile threat if he believed it would save him.

"I see you understand me," he said smoothly. "And in case your husband's life is not enough of an inducement, there is also your brother's—or had you forgotten him?"

With a guilty start, Holly realized she had. She had not thought of Noel—her dear twin—since hearing of Hunt's arrest. "What of him?"

"I have also ample evidence of his treasonous activities in France. The war will be over soon, by all accounts. 'Tis why I need these few weeks to make other plans for my own future. Your brother will wish to return to England when he can be of no further use to Napoléon."

"Noel is no traitor," she stated firmly.

"My sources say otherwise."

She would not, *could* not believe it! But if Teasdale had falsified information against Hunt, he might well have fabricated documents implicating Noel, as well.

"It seems you hold all the cards, Mr. Teasdale," she said at last. "I have only my word for the vile things you have said and done. Set against your falsified 'evidence' I suppose that would not count for much."

"You are very wise, Lady Vandover. I suspected that all along. But as I said, the war will likely be over soon. By then I intend to have begun a new life for myself, perhaps in the southern continent of America. Once I am gone, you are free to mend your fences with your husband—if you can."

At that moment Holly hated Teasdale more than she had ever known herself capable of hating. "You have made that rather doubtful. If there is justice in the world, whatever ship you board will sink to the bottom of the ocean. May your death be lingering and painful when it comes, Mr. Teasdale."

For a moment he looked almost shaken, but he recovered at once. "It is natural you should feel that way, I suppose. But while I await my demise, I recommend that you await your husband's release from a safe distance. Go back to Derbyshire, my lady. Send no letters, no messages, to Vandover. That way I will have no cause to suspect you of repenting of our agreement prematurely."

Holly's spurt of defiance evaporated, to be replaced by despair. If Teasdale told the truth, then indeed Hunt's life—and Noel's—would be safe. But her relationships with either of them could never be the same again. Her life's happiness was the sacrifice required for their lives' continuance. So be it. "I will return to Derbyshire tomorrow," she said dully, just as Reginald's returning footsteps sounded in the hall. "No letters."

"SURELY YOU CAN STAY just a few days to rest before undertaking the journey back," Reginald insisted. He still could not comprehend his sister-in-law's sudden decision to leave, especially after his mother had told him how adamant she had been at first to see Hunt. "I can carry messages to Hunt for you," he offered.

Holly shook her head, and he was struck by the tragedy in her eyes. They reminded him of a painting he had been studying by one of the masters. "No, I have realized that her grace is right." She glanced towards Camilla. "My coming was impulsive and foolish, and Hunt would be displeased if he knew of it."

The duchess nodded her agreement. "I vow, though, you must be still fatigued, Holly. But then, travelling does not seem to tire you as it does me."

"I shall be fine," Holly assured them both. "My mother still has need of me, so I'd best return to her at once. I—I hope to see you at Christmas, if not before."

After seeing her off in the carriage, Reg turned to his mother. "I still think I shall tell Hunt that she came. Despite what you say, he may find her concern cheering. This recent estrangement between them is only adding to his troubles, I'm certain."

"Estrangement?" His mother's eyes widened. "You have said nothing to me of this before, Reginald."

Already he regretted mentioning it. The duchess still cherished faint hopes that he might one day inherit, he knew, for all that she had seemed to become genuinely fond of Holly over the past year. "Just a misunderstanding, I don't doubt," he said hastily.

"Still, I cannot think it advisable that you or your father mention her visit to Hunt. Think how it will make him feel to know that she left the very next day, without trying to see him, or sending a message."

Reluctantly, Reg nodded. Holly had not wanted to leave though, he thought, remembering again the pain in her eyes.

Really, he must have her sit for a portrait sometime, so that he could capture it—not that he wanted her to remain unhappy, of course. He recalled how sprightly she had been last winter and spring, a vivid contrast to her mood of late. Then, he had thought she was just the thing for his sober brother. Grandmama had thought so, too.

"Mother, I believe I will return to Wickburn early this year," he announced suddenly. "Little is going on at the Academy right now, and Grandmama may need my support through this crisis. In her last letter she sounded a trifle despondent."

"Why certainly, my love, if you think it best," replied the duchess. "Though why you would want to immure yourself in the country when there is still an abundance of company in Town... But then you always were a considerate boy." She smiled fondly up at him. "When did you want to go?"

"Tomorrow, I think." Perhaps between them, he and Grandmama could discover a way to patch things up between Hunt and Holly.

HOLLY TRUDGED back up the hill from the village, as emptyhanded as she had been on her return every day for the past month and more.

Rain or shine, every morning after breakfast she donned her cloak and bonnet and walked to the village, hoping that she might finally receive word of Hunt's release. And every day the postmistress regretfully disappointed her.

Her only news came in the form of the London papers, which she had paid handsomely to have delivered to Tidebourne only a day after they appeared in London. But though she combed them eagerly for news of Hunt, she never found any. That was good, she supposed, for it meant that the Duke of Wickburn's influence was sufficient to prevent the spread of scandal. Unfortunately, it left her in the dark, as well. And after Teasdale's threats, she did not even dare to write to the duchess or Reginald. Gloomily, she reentered the house.

"Oh, there you are, Holly," Blanche greeted her as she hung her cloak on a peg by the door. "Maman has been asking for you this half-hour past. Something about one of the new maids—though why she thinks *you* would know when I do not is beyond my understanding!" She sniffed. "I cannot see why you find it necessary to walk to the village every day, anyway. Surely your high and mighty husband would send a messenger directly here were there any *good* news to relate."

Holly headed for the stairs without replying to consult her mother. She suspected that Blanche took a twisted pleasure in her misfortune, and she would not give her the added satisfaction of seeing how her taunts stung. She reminded herself yet again that Blanche's ill temper was founded in jealousy.

The only thing that preserved Holly's sanity during these long days of waiting was her continuing campaign to improve Tidebourne estate. Already there was a noticeable difference in the house itself. With the regular schedule she had instituted for cleaning and repairs, Tidebourne now reflected the family's importance in the district better than it had at any time in Holly's memory.

And Holly's efforts did not stop with the ordering of Tidebourne House, but extended into the village. She conferred with the rector of the parish to discover which families were most needy, and precisely what their needs were. Then she set about alleviating them. With Blanche's grudging help, she prepared parcels and baskets of food, medicines and other necessities, just as the dowager had shown her how to do at Wickburn.

Regular contact with the poorest villagers made dwelling on her own troubles impossible, Holly found. As December entered in, she had the satisfaction of knowing that this year, at least, those families would have something to be thankful for at Christmas. For the first time she began to understand the verse in Acts, "It is more blessed to give than to receive." Certainly, her giving of time and resources was benefiting her greatly—keeping other thoughts at bay while enabling her to count her blessings.

One cold grey morning, when Christmas was less than two weeks distant, Holly pulled her cloak tight against the wind as she approached the village post office. She wasn't sure why she kept coming. Blanche was right. Any good news would likely be sent by special messenger. Holly was surprised, therefore, when the postmistress greeted her enthusiastically.

"Miss Pax—er—my lady!" she exclaimed, waving a letter gleefully. "This came for you only twenty minutes ago. I was going to have Joshua carry it up to the house within the hour if you didn't come. I do hope it is what you have been waiting for!"

The postmistress was clearly curious, but Holly had not the least intention of allowing word of Hunt's disgrace to spread beyond her immediate family. Already she regretted telling Blanche.

"Thank you, Mrs. Williams," she said simply, taking the letter. "I hope so, too." A single glance showed her that it was addressed in the duchess's hand rather than her husband's. She tucked it into the pocket of her cloak, as it was far too windy to read it outdoors, and spent the short walk back steeling herself against possible bad news.

Blanche was in the parlour when she returned and asked sarcastically, as she always did, whether Holly had received a letter.

"In fact I have," she replied, sitting down to break the seal. She had intended to read it in the privacy of her room, but no matter. Whatever the news was, she would have to share it with the family soon enough.

"Oh, praise the good Lord!" exclaimed Holly a moment later, the thin sheet of paper between her fingers trembling with her relief. "Hunt has been cleared. He is free at this very moment, in fact."

"Is it from your husband, then?" asked Blanche waspishly, her small blue eyes glittering with curiosity. "Does he say why he never wrote before?"

Holly winced but bit back a retort. "No, 'tis from the duchess," she answered reluctantly, dreading her sister's smirk. "I expect I shall hear from Hunt within the week." Holly kept her voice neutral, willing herself to believe her own words.

Blanche merely sniffed. "I will believe that when I see it. The marquess would hardly have been prevented from writing to you had he *wished* it, even shut up in the King's Bench."

"So you have said numerous times," replied Holly stiffly.

Their mother bustled into the parlour just then. "I can see by your face, my love, that something momentous has occurred," she said before Holly could speak. "Have you had word from Lord Vandover?"

"Not *from* him, but of him." Her mother's enthusiasm, such a contrast to Blanche, made her smile. "He has been cleared of all charges."

"But Holly, that is marvellous!" Her mother hurried over to embrace her. "Will you be going to him now? Ring for Mary that she may help your maid to pack."

"Not so fast, Maman! I will think you wish to be rid of me." Holly clung to her smile. "The duchess said nothing of my coming to them just yet. Perhaps the duke wishes to have his son to himself over the holidays."

"But you are his *wife!*" Her mother was plainly aghast. "I should think you would want to fly instantly to his side, to help him forget the horrors of prison life. What a reunion it will be, no? So romantic!"

Holly felt the familiar ache in her throat. Once she, too, had been Gallically romantical—and not so very long ago, either. Only a year ago, in fact, though it felt like aeons.

"Hunt has had to endure few of the *physical* hardships of prison, at least," she finally said, and her words sounded cold, even to herself. "The duchess assured me when I went to London that he has been staying in what amounts to a well-appointed inn room, only nominally attached to King's Bench."

"But think you how galling it must have been for a man of his station to be deprived of his freedom for so long—not to mention the scandal involved," Mrs. Paxton insisted, echoing the very thoughts that had haunted Holly since learning of his arrest. "The woman he loves should have been the first to greet him on his return to the outside world."

"So melodramatic, Maman," said Holly faintly. "I—I had best go to consult Cook about the fish. She has promised to prepare your favourite turbot tonight." Turning away quickly before her mother could see the tears stinging her eyes, she hurried from the room.

The woman he loves. If only she were that!

Despite her disappointment that the news had come from Camilla rather than Hunt, Holly was spurred to renewed thought, and then action. Hunt was free, which meant that Teasdale had completed his arrangements for his own escape. But Holly was determined that he should not go unscathed after all he had cost her.

While she still did not quite dare to write to London, she thought of another way to possibly thwart him. Going to her chamber, she penned three identical letters, then walked to the village to post them to the authorities in Plymouth, Portsmouth and Bristol. If Teasdale hadn't left the country yet, there was a good chance he never would!

The remainder of the day passed slowly for Holly, though she tried to occupy herself with weaving greenery into wreaths for the church. In years past, these weeks before Christmas had been a special time for her and Noel. Last year it had been a time of joyful anticipation, leading up to the most wonderful day of her life. Now, despite the wonderful news of Hunt's release and her hopes of bringing Teasdale to justice, she felt strangely depressed.

The next morning, Holly and her mother were just finishing breakfast, a meal Blanche generally took in her bedchamber, when Mary bustled into the dining-room.

"Oh, Miss Holly, here you are!" Unlike Blanche, the old servant frequently forgot Holly's title, especially when she was excited. "This was just delivered by special post, so I thought you would want it at once."

"Thank you, Mary." With shaking hands, she broke the seal—Lord Vandover's seal. The address was in the strong, flowing handwriting she remembered so well. Her heart began to pound in hard, slow strokes. Holly would have much preferred to open the letter in private, but by now her mother was clamouring to know its contents.

"Read it, my love, do! He wishes you to come to him instantly, no? Quickly, *chérie,* quickly—what does he say?"

Trembling, she unfolded the single sheet.

"Madam," it read,

By now the duchess will have informed you of my release and acquittal. The dowager duchess wishes to gather the family about her at Wickburn to mark my liberation along with the holiday season. As her health has deteriorated in recent months, I shall not deny her request. You will join me there, as my wife, for the duration of the Christmas Season. I shall expect you there on Friday.

Vandover

Holly felt the colour leave her face as she read the terse, formal missive. She was reading it through for the third time, trying to glean some shred of tenderness from the words, when her mother's voice recalled her.

"Well, what does he say? Does he want you to go to him in Town? Does he wish to have a glorious reunion to celebrate his freedom?"

Holly looked up, trying to keep the bleakness in her heart from reflecting in her eyes. She forced her lips into a semblance of a smile. "He . . . he wishes me to come to Wickburn—for Christmas."

CHAPTER TWELVE

As THE CRESTED CARRIAGE made its way northwards through Yorkshire, Holly supposed she should be thankful that the clouds had not yet fulfilled their threat of more snow. These northern roads were sometimes impassable by Yuletide, she knew. Despite her misgivings about the reception that awaited her at Wickburn, she had no desire to be stranded at some inn or farmhouse along the way.

Evening was falling, along with a few ghostly flakes, when the carriage drove through the open gates of Wickburn. At the sight of the sprawling mansion atop the knoll, Holly's spirits rose. She could not help but associate Wickburn with happiness. Memories surged round her as they rolled up the long, winding drive.

She recalled last year's Christmas preparations, in tandem with those for her wedding; her wedding day—and night; those first wonderful weeks of marriage. And then last summer, the perceptible healing of the rift between Hunt and herself, cut short far too soon. Surely here, of all places, she and Hunt could finally mend the cracks in their relationship and truly become one. Especially at Christmas, the season of hope and forgiveness.

"We're here, my lady, we're here!" chattered Mabel excitedly, as she had at least a dozen times over the past half-hour. "My mum will be so happy I could come home for Christmas!"

Holly's heart lifted with an answering enthusiasm. "Your brothers and sisters will be pleased to see you, as well," she said to her abigail, who had become a friend during the long weeks in Derbyshire. "And the servants, too, of course," she added, with a wink that made Mabel blush. She had recently confided to Holly that she and Harry Tibbs, one of the upper footmen, had an understanding.

The carriage drew to a halt, the front door was thrown open and light streamed from within. With a final, deep breath, Holly stepped down from the coach to approach the imposing portal. Deeds, the butler, greeted her warmly before preceding her to the formal front drawing-room. Holly wondered if he could hear the staccato beating of her heart.

"Lady Vandover," he intoned, throwing open the double doors to the drawing-room.

A merry fire crackled on the hearth, and dozens of candles blazed in their sconces. For a moment, to Holly's dazzled eyes, the room appeared crowded, but then the faces turned towards her resolved themselves into the five she had expected to see. The duke and duchess had been sharing the small crocodile sofa farthest from the fire, while Reginald and Hunt sat on either side of the dowager duchess on the larger sofa near the hearth.

Holly's eyes went first to the dowager. It had dismayed her to learn that her beloved friend was ill, and now she was looking for signs that the dowager had aged since last summer. Certainly her personality was as strong as ever; though the gentlemen rose at Holly's entrance, it was the dowager who spoke first.

"I am so happy you have arrived ahead of the snow, dear lass," she said, her Irish lilt pronounced. "I was just reminding the others of how the road can deteriorate so quickly at this time of year, though Hunt assured me that they were still perfectly clear when he passed over them an hour since." She slanted a fond smile up at her eldest grandson.

Startled, Holly followed her glance, realizing only then that she had been delaying the moment when she must meet her husband's eyes. His features and golden brown hair looked much the same as she remembered, nor was his stance any less proud than it had ever been. But there was a shadowed, haunted expression in his clear blue eyes that made him seem a different man.

"You arrived just today?" Holly heard herself asking. It was not what she had planned as her first words to her husband, and the accusation implicit in her question made her wish immediately that she could recall it.

Hunt merely nodded, but the dowager spoke before his lack of response could become obvious. "Aye, he travelled hither with Wickburn and Camilla. She was most anxious, I believe, to be off of the roads before nightfall."

"Yes, I do detest travelling after dark, especially in wintertime," the duchess agreed. "We pressed hard, and made the journey in only four days' time."

Reginald then stepped up to embrace her, looking for all the world like a carrot in his orange coat and breeches, topped by his shock of hair of nearly the same colour. "Welcome home, sister," he drawled.

This seemed to galvanize the others, for the duke and duchess now came forward to welcome her to Wickburn and to congratulate her and each other over Hunt's acquittal. Though he managed a couplet for the occasion, Holly thought even the duke's jubilance rather forced, and wondered at it. She was acutely aware of Hunt standing alone, by the mantel.

Plainly he had not forgiven her—he seemed as distant now as he had ever been. And he had elected to travel with Camilla rather than herself. Her hopes for a reconciliation began to wither within her. Just as she felt she could bear his silence no longer, the dowager came to her rescue.

"I daresay poor Holly is fagged to death after travelling since the crack of dawn. Hunt, why do you not take her up to her room to freshen up before dinner? I'm sure you will both be glad of a few moments to be private, after two months apart," she said with a suggestive wink.

Hunt finally stepped forward to bow formally over Holly's hand. "Your servant, madam." She was chilled by the frost in his tone. He showed not the faintest glimmer of answering humour at his grandmother's teasing.

Nodding to the rest of the family with a stiff smile, Holly took her husband's proffered arm and accompanied him from the room. They walked the length of the great hall in silence, passing over its black and white marble to the elegantly curving great staircase. Instead of the thrill of admiration the vaulted arches and painted dome above had always before inspired, Holly now found the empty, echoing spaces above her oppressive.

"I'm happy to see you again, Hunt," she finally said as they mounted the first steps. Her words seemed to run away into faint whispers in the enormous hall.

His eyes met hers briefly. "I thank you for the sentiment. I am happy to be home." But he did not look happy at all.

Concern warred with the diffidence Holly felt at being alone with this man who seemed a complete stranger. Had his brief stay in prison scarred him so deeply? Or had she done this to him, with her long silence? Now, perhaps, she could begin to undo that damage—but first there were things she needed to know.

"Maman sends her congratulations on your acquittal," she continued. "Did...did they discover the identity of the real traitor?" Even now she dared not mention Teasdale's name.

He gave a quick shake of his head. "I was released owing to insufficient evidence, that is all." The look he shot her added as clearly as words—*No thanks to you.*

Holly could scarcely deny it, as it was her letter from Noel which had sent him to prison. She was determined, however, to confess at least a part of what she had done, to ask for his forgiveness. But her husband now seemed so cold and unapproachable that she scarcely knew how to begin. "Hunt, I—"

But he cut her off. "As I already wrote you, my grandmother is not well. Reginald has informed me, in fact, that the doctor gives her only weeks to live." Holly gasped faintly, but he went on as though he hadn't heard. "It is her wish that the family be gathered about her for what will most likely be her last Christmas. You will oblige me by endeavouring to behave as though everything is well between us, for her sake. With that in mind, we will occupy our usual chambers. I wished to forewarn you."

For a moment, Holly thought she detected a hint of a question in his eyes, but before she could be sure, it was gone, replaced by the shuttered look he had worn since her arrival.

"Of course," she said quickly, the questions she had planned to ask abruptly erased by the shock of hearing the doctor's prognosis. A few weeks! Holly would never have guessed she was so sick as all that.

Hunt opened the door to her suite. The garden-like sitting-room was as she remembered it, and the lilac-and-white bedchamber beyond. Involuntarily, her eye went to the dressing-room door that led to her husband's rooms.

"Feel free to lock that door if you prefer," he said, "though I can assure you that it will not be necessary. I shall leave you now to dress for dinner. The others are hungry, as Grandmama insisted that we wait the meal for you."

Torn now between grief for the dowager, who had become so dear a friend, and for her marriage, which was dying just as surely, Holly allowed him to leave without another word. Tears of reaction and despair filled her eyes. Mabel bustled in at that moment, forcing Holly to dry her eyes and turn her mind to other matters.

"Wear the rose-and-white silk, my lady," Mabel suggested, pulling it from the press, where she had already hung

Holly's gowns. It was one of her most attractive, if a bit fine for a family dinner. The eager gleam in Mabel's eyes told Holly that her abigail thought she should look her best tonight. Perhaps she was right.

"Very well, Mabel. Help me out of this one."

Once Mabel had fastened her into the gown and repinned her hair, she dismissed the girl. She needed a few moments to collect her thoughts before she went down. As she had so many times before, she attempted to imagine what it must have been like for a man like her husband to face prison and public censure, even for something he knew was the result of a mistake. Except that it *wasn't* a mistake. His arrest had been deliberately arranged by Teasdale, though it was apparently she that Hunt held responsible.

Nor could she come right out and deny guilt in the matter, until she knew what had become of Teasdale. She needed to know whether the threat he held over Hunt—and over Noel—was still valid. The clock tolled the hour, and Holly realized that she had tarried long enough. The family had waited dinner on her as it was, as Hunt had made a point of telling her.

The others were already assembled in the dining-room. If any of them thought it odd that Hunt had not waited for her, they concealed it admirably, she thought. At her entrance, the duchess took her place at one end of the long table, regal in a green silk gown that made the most of her flame red hair and white skin. The duke moved to sit opposite her, with the other four spread along the length of the table at such a distance from one another as to make conversation difficult.

"I trust you are feeling more the thing, Holly, dear," said the duchess as Holly took her seat across from Hunt. Reginald was her dinner partner, if someone five feet away could be considered as such, with the dowager across from him.

"Yes, thank you, your grace. But then, as you know, I have never found travel especially fatiguing." Out of the corner of her eye, she saw Hunt turn his head sharply at her words, though he said nothing.

"Can't think why anyone would," commented the dowager loudly from her place down the table. Though she went along with her daughter-in-law's insistence on formal family dining, she refused, as always, to limit her conversation to the person beside her. "How can sitting all day in a carriage exhaust anyone?"

The duchess primmed up her lips. "Some of us are more delicate than others. The motion of a carriage for hours on end never fails to make me feel poorly. 'Tis why I prefer to make frequent stops during a journey—though, this time I wished to reach Wickburn more quickly than usual." She flicked an almost apprehensive glance at Holly.

"I understand, of course," said Holly quickly. Shaving a day from her usual trip had probably been at Hunt's insistence. Of course, he could have come separately just as well, stopping to collect her in Derbyshire. But he had not. "My sister, Blanche, feels much the same about travelling," she added, to conceal her pain.

In fact, she *had* felt a bit ill for the first hour of today's journey, but it had passed—and she certainly would not admit now to what seemed a simple fit of nerves. The dowager's approval meant far more to her than the duchess's, especially now. She examined the dowager surreptitiously but could see no outward evidence that she was as ill as Hunt had said. Could the doctor have been mistaken?

"Would you care to hear about the painting I am working on?" Reginald asked her just then, breaking a lengthening silence. "I have improved on the usual methods of depicting a landscape, if I do say so myself."

Holly smiled gratefully at him. "I look forward to seeing it. Is it of a scene on the estate?"

They fell to discussing art as the soup was served and the company began to eat. Though she kept her face turned towards her brother-in-law, Holly's every nerve was focused on the man across from her, who had not spoken since her entrance. During the early days of their marriage, when they had been placed across from each other at table, they had spoken with their eyes if not their mouths. But tonight she could not even bring herself to look at him, to face the hostility in those eyes that had once held such affection.

"I do hope the snow holds off through tomorrow so that Anne and her family will not have difficulties on the road," said the duchess after a moment. "Christmas is not the same without children in the house."

Everyone agreed with this sentiment. "Anne is another female who travels well," commented the dowager, deliberately needling the duchess. "She gets it from me, I'll be bound."

Really, one would never guess the dowager was ill, thought Holly. What a contrast to Camilla.

"Yes, Lady Anne is quite robust," returned the duchess, making it almost an insult. "She and Holly have much in common."

Holly bit her lip, glancing involuntarily at her husband. Always before, even during their long estrangement, he had come to her defence when his stepmother aimed those little barbs at her. But not tonight.

The dowager made a sound suspiciously like a snort before turning to her son. "Wickburn, why do you not propose a toast? I should say the occasion certainly calls for it."

The duke cleared his throat and raised his glass, his eyes twinkling. As always, he appeared primarily amused at the exchange between his wife and mother. Holly doubted he had even noticed that veiled insult.

"Of course, Mother. To the triumph of Justice and Hunt's release; To a Christmas Season that's sure to please. Welcome home, son!"

Hunt scarcely drank to the toast, as it was patently to him, but he could not resist a glance in Holly's direction as she dutifully sipped. She appeared perfectly composed, he thought cynically, not the least bit discomfited at drinking a toast to his freedom from an imprisonment he owed entirely to her. The wine, the finest from the Wickburn cellars, tasted like vinegar in his mouth.

He had been in a foul humour all day. Travelling with his stepmother was never pleasant—her constant complaints about her health, the stops and the condition of the roads nearly drove him mad. After nearly two months of enforced inactivity, though, he could not ride for long at a stretch and had perforce to listen to much of it. Relieved as he was to be free, there had been moments when he wondered whether it were worth the price.

And now he had to face Holly again. During his confinement—as luxurious a confinement as money could buy, but confinement nonetheless—he had laboured to uproot all tenderness for his wife from his soul. He'd thought he had succeeded, right up until the moment he saw her again. But after one glimpse of her face he had known he was in peril of falling in love with her all over again.

Sternly he reminded himself of how she had deceived him, how she had not even troubled to write to him during his imprisonment. It helped a little. At the very least, it enabled him to keep his voice and face impassive when he glanced across the table at her again.

She was even more beautiful than he remembered, her long black hair sweeping down to frame her ivory face before it was looped up behind in an intricate knot. Irresistibly, he was reminded of the first time he saw her, at Lady Chittendon's ball more than a year ago. In spite of everything that had gone since, he felt even more drawn to her now than he had been then.

During the remainder of the meal, Hunt determinedly engaged his grandmother in a conversation about the tenant families and their prospects for the coming year. It was a subject about which both of them felt strongly, and served—almost—to distract him from the woman across the table.

"The Kellers lost the best of their two milk cows in October," the dowager was saying. "'Twill be a difficult winter for them, I fear. Their farmland has never produced much, rocky as it is."

"I will visit them tomorrow, to see what can be contrived," Hunt said, a bit more loudly than necessary. "Perhaps the Grants would be willing to exchange a heifer for a few of those acres. Mr. Grant spoke to me last summer about wishing to expand his barley crop."

His grandmother nodded. "Have you given any thought to the Feast of St. Stephen? The tenants will be looking forward to a grand celebration, with you at home again."

Hunt suddenly remembered last year, when that holiday had fallen only two days after his wedding. He and Holly, filled with the euphoria of their new union, had gone themselves to hand out gifts to the tenants, staying to drink cider, watch the mumming plays and dance to the tune of old Mr. Wilson's fiddle. It had been one of the happiest days of his life, he thought now.

"Certainly, we must do something special," he finally answered. "I will think on it, Grandmama."

Though Hunt had never cared much for the custom of remaining with his father and brother over port, tonight he saw the ladies depart with relief. Thinking ahead to the moment when he would be sleeping—or trying to sleep—only one room away from Holly, he applied himself to the bottle with vigour.

"I'd been meaning to ask you, brother," said Reginald, when the men were alone at the enormous table. "Did the Foreign Office ever discover which one of the servants hid that letter in your house? Or was it connected to the real traitor at all?"

"I...don't believe it was," replied Hunt carefully.

"Whole thing was a tempest in a teapot, if you ask me," declared the duke. "Said so at the very beginning. I heard what that letter said after they deciphered it—sounded like a billet-doux to one of the maids from her lover."

Reg laughed. "No, really? A love letter?" He turned back to Hunt and immediately the laughter left his face, to be replaced by concern.

"Yes, that is what it sounded like," Hunt agreed, not meeting his brother's eyes. He realized that he would rather believe Holly a traitor to England than to their marriage.

During the inquest, he had convinced himself that he merely wished to avoid the scandal that would result if it became known that the Marchioness of Vandover was a traitoress. But now he suspected that he had, in fact, had another motive for his silence.

He motioned for the footman to refill his glass.

"THE SNOW seems to have stopped for the moment," Holly observed from her post by the drawing-room window. She felt far too unsettled to sit. Tonight she would surely have an opportunity to ask Hunt about Teasdale—and then to tell him as much of the truth as she dared. How would he react?

"Anne should be here by early afternoon, if the weather holds tomorrow," said the dowager, moving a bit away from the fire, where Holly had insisted she sit.

"Yes, the children will be clamouring to be here in good time for the festivities," agreed the duchess, spreading her silken skirts into a picturesque arrangement on the other sofa. "Monday will be the mistletoe hunt, and they would never miss that."

Unbidden, a memory came to Holly of last year's mistletoe hunt, when she and Hunt had found themselves briefly alone in the woods and he had stolen a quick kiss. She had been so carefree then, looking forward to her marriage with happy anticipation. She shivered suddenly.

"Are you, Holly?" asked the duchess, in the tone of one repeating a question.

"I beg pardon, your grace! I fear I was wool-gathering," said Holly hastily, turning from the window.

"I was concerned that you are not feeling quite the thing tonight, despite your protestations at dinner that travelling did not tire you." She slid a look at the dowager as she spoke.

"No, I feel perfectly well, your grace. I was merely daydreaming."

"Of tonight, I doubt not," said the dowager with a chuckle. "We'll not be offended if you youngsters wish to retire early, shall we, Camilla?"

The duchess's mouth tightened ever so slightly. "Of course not."

Unable to smile, Holly turned back to her contemplation of the wintry darkness that seemed to reflect her own bleak expectations for the future.

A hum of voices gave her a moment's warning before the gentlemen entered the room. The duke came in first, followed closely by Reginald. Hunt followed more slowly, as though reluctant to join them—or her.

"We were beginning to despair of you," said the duchess, offering a smooth cheek for her husband's kiss, and then her son's. "I trust you haven't drunken yourselves insensible."

Wickburn and Reginald seated themselves on either side of her, while Hunt moved to join the dowager by the fire.

"Hunt was the only two-bottle man at the table tonight," said Reginald. "I daresay he has cause enough, though. I'd wish to forget the past two months, as well, if I were he." He shuddered expressively.

Holly darted a quick glance at her husband, where he was fully engaged in spreading a rug over his grandmother's lap.

"Now, Hunt, you can fuss over me anytime," the dowager admonished him. "I was saying to Holly not ten minutes ago that none of us oldsters would find it amiss if the two of you preferred to make it an early night tonight. Why do you not take your wife up to bed?"

Holly braced herself for his refusal, but it did not come.

"An excellent thought, Grandmama," he said pleasantly. "My wife and I are quite overdue for our reunion, are we not? Two months is a very long time."

The smile curving his lips did not reach his eyes, but Holly doubted anyone else in the room noticed it. To all outward appearances, he was every inch the ardent, attentive husband. He put one arm about her shoulders and drew her to his side, but there was no warmth in his touch.

For a wild moment, Holly wanted to protest, to remain below with the others, where it was safe, rather than go upstairs alone with this stranger her husband had become. But of course that was absurd. She forced herself to assume an artificial smile, much like Hunt's.

"A very long time indeed, my lord," she said, keeping the quaver she felt from her voice.

Hunt's smile broadened, though his eyes glittered dangerously, with wine, and perhaps with something else she could not decipher. "Then shall we to bed, my lady?"

CHAPTER THIRTEEN

IF HOLLY had been uncomfortable going upstairs with Hunt earlier, she was now far more so. She was beginning to fully realize just how deep her husband's animosity towards her went. It was up to her to set things right. As they approached the door to her boudoir Holly moistened her lips, but before she could frame a suitable opening phrase, Hunt spoke.

"For a moment I thought you meant to refuse to accompany me. It is well you did not. I am determined that my grandmother's final days be good ones. I owe her that much, at the very least, after all she has done for me. If it pleases her to think us a happy couple, a happy couple we will contrive to appear. You will help me to give her that final gift." It was a statement, not a request.

Holly closed her eyes for a moment against another stab of sorrow. The dowager had taught her far more, both about running an estate and about life itself, than her own mother had ever done. During the evening, the dowager's brave performance had nearly convinced her that the spirited old lady would recover, that the doctor had been wrong. Hunt was speaking again, and she sternly suppressed her tears to look at him.

"I see my plan disgusts you." His mouth twisted cynically. "No matter. You are my wife and will do as I bid, for this fortnight, at least."

Though she had intended to be conciliatory, Holly glared at him. "I have as great a desire as you to make the dowager happy. However, if you wish me to portray a loving, contented wife, you would do well to consider your own performance, as well, my lord," she snapped. "Do you suppose that your grandmother does not see how you act towards me? She is not a stupid woman, you know!"

Hunt blinked as though her show of spirit startled him, but then his jaw tightened. When he finally spoke, his words dripped ice. "Your desires are of no concern to me and I take no responsibility for them whatsoever. Your person is another matter, and still under my control. I want your word that you will do all in your power to preserve the fiction that all is well between us while we remain at Wickburn—that you will do nothing to cause the dowager greater pain."

"Of course," said Holly, her anger evaporating as quickly as it had appeared. "I—I care deeply for her, too, you know."

"Then you have an inducement beyond your *given word* to play along." His smile was still mirthless, but now a flame, perhaps of anger, danced behind his eyes.

"There is another thing." He reached past her to open the door to her suite, then motioned her to enter. "My grandmother has more than once expressed a desire to see an heir to Wickburn before she dies. It is unlikely now that she will have that wish. Still, it would doubtless bring her comfort to be assured that one will make his appearance in the near future."

Holly's heart hammered as he followed her into the room, hope and a vague fear warring within her. "So much for your fine promises that I might lock the door," she retorted, striving to subdue the quaver in her voice. "And yet you choose to doubt *my* word?"

He took a step closer to her so that she could hear his rapid breathing and smell the warm scent of him that she remembered so well. "Don't worry," he said softly, his voice sending shivers down her spine, but whether of fear or anticipation she could not be sure. "I do not intend to ravish you. I merely wished you to understand that I'll not shirk my duty in this matter, nor allow you to shirk yours."

He turned abruptly away from her as he continued. "After the Christmas season, I shall return to London. You may come with me if you wish, or go to your mother. In any case, we need have little to do with each other, save what contact is necessary to fulfil that duty. The sooner we get an heir, the sooner we can part to follow our own lives. If that can be accomplished during this fortnight, we need never see each other again."

With that, he left the room, pulling the door behind him. A moment later, Holly heard the door of his chamber open and close, and then silence.

HUNT STOOD STOCK-STILL in the middle of his own room, breathing hard. What the devil had he been about to say that about producing an heir? That was not a part of his plan. The dowager had not said so much as a word about it to him since his arrival. Nor was an heir an absolute necessity, since there was Reginald as well as Anne's two sons to inherit if he should remain childless.

But when Holly had stood before him, breathtaking in her sudden anger, his desire for her had overwhelmed his reason. The wine he had overindulged in at dinner had likely played a part as well, he reflected wryly as his pulse slowly returned to normal.

Absently, Hunt began to unknot his cravat, unwilling just yet to ring for his valet. Weeks of frustrating idleness had given him ample time for thought—far too much time, in fact. Now he wondered if the elaborate scenario of deceit he had worked out while in prison was simply the product of boredom combined with an overactive imagination.

Holly had originally married him, he'd decided, in order to have access to secret information from the Foreign Office; she had spied on him all along, possibly copying documents from his desk when he was away. After he caught her burning a message from her superiors, she had fostered the coolness between them to avoid giving explanations. Then, when he had caught her returning from a secret, treasonous meeting, she had deliberately placed that letter to be found, making certain that it contained no information that would be useful to the authorities.

But just now, when he had looked into Holly's wide green eyes, all those suspicions had suddenly seemed vaguely absurd. The only thing he knew for certain was that she had received letters from France. They might even have been from a relative, he supposed, rather than a lover. Other than those letters and her secrecy about them, he knew of nothing Holly had ever done to betray his trust.

If she were innocent, though, why had she not come to London the moment she heard of his arrest to dispute the charges? Surely she'd have come if she really cared. Whatever secret she was keeping had to be more important to her than her husband's life.

Why had he not demanded the truth from her just now?

Because he was afraid, he realized. Afraid of what her answer would be—afraid of losing her. Whatever she had done, however little she cared for him, he still desired her and—yes, he could no longer deny it—still loved her. And now, with his brutish ultimatums, he had pushed her further away than ever.

He stared for a moment at the door that separated their chambers, then crossed swiftly to it. Perhaps he could still undo the damage....

From the other side of the door, he heard a faint noise. Pressing his ear to the panel, he deciphered the soft sound of sobbing. Holly was crying. Something inside him twisted, hurting him. He reached for the doorknob.

No, he had done enough damage already tonight. If he went in there now, saw her huge green eyes wet with tears, her long black hair falling about her shoulders, he might well ravish her, after all. After what he had just said to her, he had no confidence in his ability to control himself. And still, there was the distinct possibility that she *did* merit some of his suspicions.

He would take things slowly, regaining her trust while gauging whether she deserved his. Then, perhaps, she would finally tell him the truth about those blasted letters that had led to so much trouble. Slowly, reluctantly, he dropped his hand to his side and moved away from the dressing-room door to ring for his valet.

WHEN HOLLY AWOKE the next morning, her eyes felt gritty and her nose swollen. Not since the day she'd left London after Teasdale's last threats had she indulged in such a protracted bout of crying. She had managed to suppress her tears briefly when Mabel came in to help her undress, but the moment the maid left, they had flowed anew, from an apparently inexhaustible source.

A part of her had died last night. She had been so certain that she could make things right with Hunt, that if only she explained and apologized he would forgive her. But now it seemed plain that she had lost Hunt's love along with his trust through her silence.

Still, she would have to try. But first she needed information. If Hunt remained unapproachable she might be able to discover what she needed to from the dowager, or Reginald. Rising, she rang for Mabel.

When she went down a short time later, she found everyone but the dowager at breakfast. Reginald, clad today in varying shades of pink, rose quickly to hold her chair while the duke and duchess bid her a good morning. Hunt nodded, but said nothing.

"I trust you slept well, my dear," said the duchess, her eyes sharp as they roved over Holly's face.

"Yes, your grace, I thank you." She was glad she had not given in to the temptation of more tears—last night's had left ravages enough. Hunt was watching her, too. Did he notice? Did he care?

A footman efficiently filled a plate from the sideboard and placed it before her. Holly regarded it uneasily. She did not think she could eat a thing. Her appetite had been off most mornings of late, and even more so today—but if she did not eat, the duchess would be certain to notice and perhaps to demand explanations. Holly picked up a piece of toast and nibbled at it halfheartedly, willing her faint queasiness to subside.

"Looks like snow," remarked the duke. "Do you still intend to ride round the estate today, son?"

"Later, perhaps," replied Hunt. Holly could feel his eyes on her, but she kept her own focused on her plate.

"Oh, Holly, I nearly forgot," said Reginald then. "Grandmama wants you to come talk to her this morning. Something about the Christmas preparations, I think."

"Oh...of course. I'll go up to her rooms now." Holly was glad of an excuse to leave her scarcely touched breakfast, though she would rather have liked to hear her husband's voice again, now that it was not angry. But this would give her an opportunity to ferret information out of his grandmother.

The dowager inhabited an imposing suite of rooms on the second floor, the same ones she had used before her husband, the old duke, had died. There had never been any question of her removing to the dower house, as she was so integral to the management of the household.

At Holly's tap, she called out at once for her to enter.

"Good morning, my dear." The dowager greeted her brightly from the chaise longue where she reclined under a light rug. Again Holly was struck by the difference between the way the dowager faced a serious illness and the way Camilla faced trifling or nonexistent ones. "I trust you rested well?"

"Very well, Grandmama, thank you." Holly had to smile at the old woman's waggling eyebrows, despite the pang she felt at recalling what had actually occurred between Hunt and herself last night. "You wished to speak with me?"

"Yes, dear. Have a seat, do." As Holly pulled a chair near to her, the dowager asked abruptly, "What do you know about what went on in London, after Hunt's arrest?"

Holly stopped in the act of seating herself to stare. "After…nothing, your grace. That is, the duchess wrote to tell me Hunt had been accused of treason, and later that he had been cleared of all charges. But I know none of the details." She wondered whether Reginald had told the dowager about her arrival in London and equally rapid departure.

"Did Hunt not write to you at all?"

Holly shook her head before remembering that the dowager was not to know how things stood between them. "Not…not of anything pertaining to the case," she qualified quickly.

"I see." The old woman's eyes were as bright as they'd ever been. "Then I suppose you are no more able than the rest of them to tell me why Hunt refused make a statement in his defence. At Wickburn's behest I wrote to him, encouraging him to be open with the investigators, but apparently to no avail. 'Tis the reason he remained there so long."

This was news to Holly. "Do you mean that Hunt was cleared despite his refusal to defend himself?" she prompted, mainly to distract her thoughts. The reason for that refusal seemed painfully clear to her, for Hunt must have known that the letter belonged to her. Her heart swelled to think that he had protected her, even after everything, at such grave danger to himself.

"Yes, once the letter was translated—and it took a small army of agents to do it, I understand—they found nothing in it to justify holding him longer. However, being of an insatiably curious disposition, I still wished to know *why* he remained silent for so long."

Holly had to smile, and not only because this information gave her hope that Hunt still cared for her. Curiosity was one more thing she and the dowager had in common, it appeared—though she doubted it had ever landed the dowager into the sort of trouble it had herself.

The dowager now leaned forward to place a dry, papery hand on Holly's knee. "Hunt's name is cleared now, but I can tell that the whole business still preys upon his mind. Only you have the power to make him forget it, my dear. Will you try to do so?"

Holly swallowed. More than ever she wished she could pour out the whole truth to this wise old woman who loved Hunt as much as she did. Her own power over her husband was now far less than his grandmother's, but of course she could not say so. Instead, she forced herself to meet the dowager's eyes, hiding the pain in her own.

"Yes. I will try."

The dowager sat back and smiled, apparently satisfied. "You ease my mind, dear. I do believe— But here are my two favourite young men. Good morning Hunt, Reginald."

Turning, Holly found her husband's eyes on her, his expression inscrutable.

"Good morning, Grandmama," said Reginald cheerily, then turned to Holly. "I am glad to find you still here, sister. Hunt says he and Grandmama need to discuss some estate business or other." He made a moue of distaste. "I, however, am going out to sketch from the hill above the river, as I mentioned last night. Would you care to come along?"

"Certainly." Time spent out in the air might help to clear her mind—and this would be an excellent chance to ask Reginald about Teasdale. "That is, if you have no other plans for me, my lord?'' she asked Hunt belatedly, recalling his attitude last night.

He glanced at her, then away, his eyes shadowed. ''If it pleases you, go. You need not ask my permission, you know.''

Holly bit her lip, hesitating, then sighed. ''Thank you, my lord. Good morning, Grandmama.'' With a quick curtsy, she left them.

After a moment, the dowager remarked to her grandson, '' 'Twill not hurt my feelings if you wish to go with them, you know. The accounts can wait.''

Hunt frowned, but then caught himself and smiled instead. He had not meant to speak so curtly to Holly, especially before his grandmother, but it had stung to see how eager she was to remove herself from his presence.

''No, I haven't the patience to watch Reg at his dabbling, as you know very well. I would only make some disparaging remark and hurt his artistic feelings.''

The dowager nodded, though her eyes sparkled with comprehension. ''Likely they will be back soon, anyway. The sky is remarkably dark for ten o'clock. I doubt the weather will hold much longer.''

Hunt agreed absently, glancing at the window. ''But let us get back to the matter at hand.'' He became suddenly brisk, ignoring the twinkle in his grandmother's eyes. ''You were going to tell me about the Bartons' sheep, were you not?''

THE AIR WAS AS FRESH as Holly could have asked for, but it was Reginald's chatter more than the cold wind stinging her cheeks that she found soothing. As they walked, he expounded at length about various artists and styles, requiring nothing in the way of a response and leaving her free to marshal her thoughts.

Hunt had looked far less angry this morning. Perhaps it was merely his grandmother's presence that held him in check, but there had been something in his expression that gave her hope. And surely his refusal to implicate her over the letter was evidence that he still cared. She had to find a way to thank him for that.

A few flakes of snow drifted past as Reginald set up his easel, but he appeared not to notice. "This is the prospect I told you of," he commented with a grandiose sweep of his arm. "I have painted it six times in as many weeks, in water and oil. Today I want to try charcoal. I saw an exhibition this autumn at the Academy that greatly inspired me." He began to trace the contours of the landscape with quick sure strokes.

Holly watched with dawning respect as the panorama before them was duplicated in miniature in black and white. Really, Reginald had quite a gift. It was so easy to dismiss him, with his dandified dress and hyperbolic speech, that she had not before considered that he might truly be a talented artist.

But though he was now working in earnest, his whole attention apparently on the paper before him, Reginald continued to talk. "Grandmama told me last night that she feels better already with her family—her happy family—about her again." The snow increased its pace, large flakes falling ever more thickly, but Reginald did not appear to notice. "I have found that happiness can be rather contagious, just as sorrow, or fear, can be."

He spoke casually, almost absent-mindedly, but Holly darted a piercing look at his face. Not by the slightest sign did he betray that his words held any special meaning. "Yes, I can see how that might be," she conceded quietly.

"Then you agree that we must surround Grandmama with as much happiness as possible. It is a strong tonic. Who knows but that with enough of it we may even prove the doctor's prognosis wrong."

"I pray that might be so." Holly suspected even more strongly that Reginald was speaking of her situation with Hunt.

The snow was coming down harder now, but instead of pausing in his artwork, Reginald seemed to be experimenting with the different effects he could produce with his charcoal stick on the wet and dry areas of his drawing. Glancing down, Holly saw that her muff and cloak were nearly white. She stamped her feet to shake the accumulation from her boots, realizing that their time outdoors could not last much longer.

"How were our friends when you left London?" she asked as casually as she could manage. "I think often of the people I met there—Lady Castlereagh, Miss Simpson..." She could not quite bring herself to mention Teasdale by name.

"Oh, did you not know?" asked Reginald, still sketching busily. "I left a mere day after you did. I have been at Wickburn this month and more."

"And you have not...corresponded with any of your particular friends? With Mr. Teasdale, for instance?" There! She had said it.

But Reginald shook his head. "Never been much of a letter writer, I'm afraid, and Teasdale's no better. One reason we lost touch for so long. But why do you ask?"

A sudden clamour from the direction of the mansion saved her from answering. A carriage had drawn up and discharged its passengers before the main entrance and the high clear voices of children drifted up to them on the wintry air.

"Lady Anne and her family have arrived, I believe," Holly said unnecessarily. Reginald had already lapsed back into his work, so she spoke softly, not wishing to startle the artist and risk ruining what looked to her inexperienced eye to be a remarkably good picture.

"Just as well." Rather to her dismay, Reginald tore the paper roughly from the pad and folded it, with little regard for the artwork. "There is too much snow for the effect I wanted. I must try this again when it does not fall so thick. Come!"

He did not appear in least put out to have wasted three-quarters of an hour's work and smiled as he offered her one arm, having tucked the easel and tablet under the other. Nor did he ask her again about her curiosity concerning Teasdale, for which she was grateful. Plainly, Reginald could give her no information, which left her again with the prospect of asking Hunt.

Their footing was slippery as they headed back, but not nearly so slippery, Holly thought, as the emotional path she had yet to tread. She only hoped she might manage to navigate that one as well as this.

CHAPTER FOURTEEN

HUNT FOUND THE BUSTLE attending the arrival of his sister and her family a welcome distraction. Despite his best intentions, he had been unable to focus on the estate business, and his grandmother had finally dismissed him with a wink that had only emphasized the gulf that still yawned between him and his wife.

In contrast, Lady Anne threw herself into his arms the moment she saw him.

"Oh, Hunt, my darling, I was never happier in my life than when I received word of your acquittal! I was frightened to death for you, I vow, for I have heard how these wartime trials are, with little regard for the evidence. Pray believe that were it not for the children I should have come to London myself to plead your case!"

He returned her embrace, trying to ignore the pain her words caused him. Holly had had no such excuse—and her pleading could have carried far more weight than Anne's. "'Tis all over now, Annie, and I'm safe home again. I've nearly convinced myself 'twas no more than a hideous nightmare. The worst of it is that I missed the hunting season!"

She laughed at that, finally releasing him so that Sir Philip and the children could come forward to offer their congratulations on his release.

Five-year-old Alice's eyes were very wide as she asked, "Did you meet many highwaymen in prison, Uncle Hunt?"

This drew a general chuckle, and Hunt assured her, along with six-year-old Michael and eight-year-old William, that he had not come into contact with any criminals whatsoever, as he had had a private room.

William, in particular, seemed quite disappointed at this news, but shook his uncle's hand and said that he was happy he was free nonetheless. "For now you can show me how to hunt foxes, as you promised last Christmas you would when I was older."

Hunt ruffled his nephew's hair. "I meant a bit older than eight, Billy boy." The lad's face fell and he said quickly, "We could not hunt this year at any rate, with all this snow on the ground. But I can show you a capital hill for sledding."

William grinned, and then within moments he and his younger siblings all began to beg to be allowed to sled before dinnertime that very day. Hunt and Anne were working out the details of the day's outdoor activity schedule when Reginald and Holly came in to join the boisterous group.

Reginald was immediately pounced upon by his niece and nephews, for he had a reputation for concealing sweets in his pockets and was always a great favourite with them. Hunt scarcely noticed their defection, for his eyes were on his wife.

Holly's eyes sparkled like emeralds and her cheeks and lips glowed from the cold, forcibly reminding him of the day he nicknamed her Holly Berry—their wedding day. Just now, her mouth looked so rosy and ripe for kissing that a shudder ran through him. Fortunately, she seemed to be finding the children as much of a distraction as he had, and did not immediately look in his direction.

"Why, you have grown half a foot since last Christmas, William, and so has Michael—what distinguished gentlemen you are both become. And Alice! Surely this beautiful young lady is never little Alice? Come give your Aunt Holly a hug." Without the least regard for dignity, Holly sat right down on the Aubusson carpet and pulled the little girl into her lap for an embrace.

Bemused, Hunt wondered why he had not noticed before how good Holly was with children. Of course, other than the few hectic days following their wedding, there had been little opportunity to observe her with any, he supposed. Somehow, though, the discovery did not surprise him.

The thought of Holly and children suddenly brought to mind the words he had spoken to her last night. His grandmother might not care greatly whether he and Holly produced an heir, but all at once he realized that he himself did. He very much wanted an heir—and from Holly. What a good mother she would be.

Unexpectedly, a lump formed in his throat, and Hunt hurriedly looked away—only to find the dowager regarding him with a most knowing expression in her twinkling blue eyes.

HOLLY BURIED HER FACE in Alice's sweet-smelling brown hair as the little girl willingly gave her a hug, grateful for the excuse to keep her eyes averted from her husband's. For just the barest moment she allowed herself the fantasy of pretending that this was her child, hers and Hunt's. A sudden longing that she had never felt before sprang up within her—a void that clamoured to be filled.

"You look positively blooming, Holly!" exclaimed Lady Anne as Alice disengaged herself to join the boys at Reginald's side. "Wintertime agrees with you, I must say—or perhaps it is Hunt's release that has put you in such good looks!"

She accompanied her remark with a broad wink that reminded Holly of the dowager. Anne had her grandmother's twinkling blue eyes, just as the duke and Hunt did, along with her brother's golden brown hair. Though she was not precisely a beauty, there was a vivacity about Lady Anne that gave her features a most attractive animation.

Holly returned her smile, though her sister-in-law's words caused a twinge at her heart. "I have always loved the wintertime, it is true," she admitted, "especially when it brings families together for Christmas." She darted a shy glance at Hunt as she spoke and was startled to find his eyes on her. Before she could fathom his expression, he turned away.

"We've brought family and to spare along," said Anne with a laugh. "Trust the children to make this Christmas a rollicking one, if not so gay as last year's festivities. Is your family to join us from Derbyshire?"

"No, my mother preferred to remain at home," replied Holly quickly, willing her colour not to change. For the first time, it occurred to her how odd it might look that they had not been invited.

Lady Anne continued, undaunted. "Is your brother not yet returned from Upper Canada, then? I should think your mother will find that event nearly as great a cause for rejoicing as we are finding this one." She gazed fondly at her own brother. "Are you and he close?" she asked then, turning back to Holly.

For a wild moment, Holly thought Lady Anne meant she and Hunt. Luckily, before she could begin stammering a reply, the real meaning of the question filtered through to her. "Oh...yes. Noel and I are twins, you see."

"Twins! I never knew that. How interesting. And with birthdays on Christmas Eve...ah, I see it now! Holly and Noel—how very clever of your parents, to be sure."

Holly regarded Anne's vivid face dubiously. She had always thought the compromise her parents had come to in their choice of names for them—one English, one French and both Christmassy—a bit trite. But Anne appeared sincere enough.

"Clever? I suppose so," Holly managed to say, conscious of Hunt where he stood listening. "As twins, we spent an inordinate amount of time together as children, especially during holidays. I must admit that I miss him more than ever at Christmas."

"Yes, I would imagine so," said Anne sympathetically. "But last I heard, much of the fighting there had moved south, so perhaps he is in no real danger now."

Holly nodded, hoping that the sentiment might prove true. Indeed, the most recent news she had read of the war with France was far more encouraging than that from America. Even now, the papers said, peace negotiations were being discussed.

"I pray not," she managed to say. "He was safe three months since, for he wrote to tell me so," she began, then stopped, appalled at how close she had come to confiding in Lady Anne. "Ah, it looks as though everyone is moving into the drawing-room for hot punch, and I suspect the children would be glad of some chocolate or cider, would they not?" she asked, standing abruptly.

THE REMAINDER OF THAT DAY was so filled with activity that Holly had no time to examine the disordered state of her emotions. With Christmas Day only a week away, the excitement of the children was contagious, and the adults entered into the preparations with enthusiasm. At Wickburn, Holly found, the decorating was by no means left to the servants, and she was glad of it.

Still, Christmases past occasionally intruded as she helped the dowager and Lady Anne to sort through the red velvet ribbons. Together, she and Anne placed candles throughout the mansion and showed the children how to tie holly and ivy onto wreaths. Instead of making her melancholy, the sense of ongoing tradition, unchanged through the years, gave Holly a comforting sense of being a part of that continuity. Her own problems seemed less overwhelming when set against that backdrop.

As she prepared for bed that night, Holly wondered when, or if, Hunt would come to her room to perform the "duty" he had spoken of the night before. She knew he had chosen his words deliberately to hurt her, but still she found herself hoping that he would fulfil them. Through the act of joining, surely she could make him understand that she loved him, that he could trust her.

Just then, she heard his footstep in the hall. Without giving herself time to think, she went swiftly to the door and opened it.

"My lord? Might... might I have a word with you?"

Hunt halted, his hand already on the handle of his own door. The guarded look was back, but she thought she detected a softening around his mouth as he took in her appearance. Suddenly realizing how she must look in her diaphanous wrapper, her hair already unbound, Holly fought down a belated surge of embarrassment.

"I, ah... that is, Duchess Aileen told me something of what you went through in London. I wished to thank you for what you did," she said in a rush.

A spasm seemed to cross his face, but then his expression hardened, the shutters back in place. "I followed the only course open to me. To have done otherwise would have further damaged the family name."

Though his voice was cold, his eyes seared her with his pain—pain that she had caused him. She suddenly realized that her thanks must have sounded to him like a confession of guilt. He turned back towards his room but she spoke again, desperately.

"I have not yet had an opportunity to ask after our acquaintances in London," she said, striving for a casual a tone. "Have they all left Town by now?"

He frowned, not surprisingly. How inane she must have sounded! "I would expect most of them have, yes," he replied.

"To include Reginald's friend, Mr. Teasdale?" No matter how the question sounded to him, she had to know. Once Teasdale was gone she could safely tell him everything.

Hunt's frown deepened, making her wonder nervously whether Reginald had mentioned her earlier questions to him. "Teasdale? I did not know you were particularly acquainted with him."

"Oh, Reginald introduced us at one of my first diplomatic evenings and we struck up quite a friendship," she improvised. "He said something about leaving for the country I believe. . . ." She trailed off as inspiration left her.

"Teasdale has left the Foreign Office," said Hunt, his features even more rigid than before. "The story he gave out was that his father needed him at the family estate. I saw no reason to doubt it at the time, but I believe I understand now why he might have found his position there . . . awkward. Thank you for enlightening me, madam."

Holly gaped at him. "What? You think that Teasdale and I—? Oh! 'Tis too absurd!" Outraged and shocked though she was, she almost laughed.

"Absurd? Is it also absurd that I should expect an explanation for that damned letter, the one that sent me to prison? If it was not from Teasdale, who was it from?"

Her brief spurt of amusement evaporated. If she told him it was from Noel, he would want the particulars. Could she be certain that Teasdale had not planted information somewhere that would imply Noel was working for the French? Once she might have trusted Hunt's affection for her to protect Noel in such a circumstance—but now?

She hesitated too long. Before she could decide how much to tell him, Hunt made her a stiff half bow and disappeared into his chamber. Impulsively, Holly started to follow him but stopped at the sound of the bell signalling his valet.

Quickly, she retreated into her room before his man came, cursing herself for the way she had bungled the interview. Still, she could not completely despair. Hunt's very jealousy showed that he yet cared for her, at least a little. In spite of her failure to clear the air between them, she slept better than she had expected.

THE NEXT DAY was Sunday, which meant time out from the bustle and more opportunity for thought, but Holly tried hard to cling to the holiday spirit. The dowager, she noticed, had brightened visibly with the arrival of Lady Anne and her children, giving her a distinct illusion of health. She was determined to do all in her power to keep the old woman's spirits up. As Reginald had said yesterday, happiness was a stronger tonic than any the doctor might prescribe.

Standing beside her husband in the same chapel where they had been married, joining their voices with those of family and villagers to sing "Joy to the World," she found it surprisingly easy to pretend that all was well between them. Perhaps, she thought, just perhaps, if she and Hunt played their parts well enough to convince the dowager that they were in love, they might begin to persuade themselves, as well.

As the song ended, she dared a glance up at Hunt, standing so close beside her that his cloak brushed her shoulder. He slanted a look back at her with what might have been a ghost of a wink. Even though she had probably imagined it, Holly felt a delicious warmth spreading through her in response.

That warmth lasted through the rest of the day, despite the fact that after the service Hunt spoke no more to her than civility demanded.

"If the weather holds fair, 'twill be a cold night," remarked the dowager at dinner. The addition of Lady Anne and Sir Philip to the party made for less empty space at the table. "Little William was asking me this afternoon about the prospects for skating."

"Perhaps we might flood the low pasture behind the orchard as we did when we were children," suggested Hunt.

"I doubt Annie will want him to try the pond, even if it freezes to the centre."

His sister shuddered. "I should say not! I'll never forget the time I fell through that ice as a child. Do you skate, Holly?"

Holly replied that she had done so on a few occasions in her youth. "I may well have forgotten how by now, though."

"In that case, we'll have to reteach you," said Hunt. His tone, as well as his look, was pleasant, if not loverlike.

Perhaps he was merely playing his role for the dowager, but Holly took hope from it nonetheless. "I shall look forward to that," she said.

He did not come to her room that night, and Holly made no further attempt to speak to him, but her spirits remained high as she changed out of her gown and into her nightdress, then unpinned her hair, unwilling to ring for Mabel. Sitting at the dressing-table and brushing out her long locks, she gazed dreamily into the mirror. Hunt had not been nearly so cold towards her today. And tomorrow would be the mistletoe hunt....

It was Christmas, the season of miracles. It was going to be all right. Somehow, she was convinced, everything was going to be all right.

BEFORE EVERYONE had even breakfasted the next morning, the children were clamouring to begin the search for mistletoe. Hunt entered into their enthusiasm determinedly, in an attempt to suppress his wildly conflicting feelings towards Holly.

"William, do you remember which trees we were lucky with last year?" he asked his nephew as the party gathered in the Great Hall.

"Of course. Are we going all together, or shall we split into teams, Uncle Hunt? May I be on yours?"

The other two children began calling out who they wanted on their teams, as well, but the dowager raised her hands for silence and they subsided.

"As I shall be the judge of who brings in the most mistletoe, I shall choose the teams. Suppose you go out two by two? Reginald, Anne, Philip, suppose each of you take one of the children. Hunt and Holly may make the fourth team."

At once William protested. "But Uncle Hunt and I were already planning our strategy! It isn't fair!"

Hunt was quick to agree. He had no wish to be alone with Holly, tormented by the memories of last year—not until he had sorted out his feelings. "Perhaps larger teams are in order," he said. "William may be on my team, as he wishes. Father and Reggie can take Alice, and Michael may go with his parents. Do you come, Camilla?"

"I believe I will," she said, to his surprise. Though the mistletoe hunt was an old Wickburn tradition dating from his father's youth, he could never recall her taking part in it. "I'll be a part of your team, Hunt, if you do not mind. Wickburn and Reggie will not wish to proceed at my pace, I know."

Hunt nodded reluctantly, knowing that William would not care to go slowly, either. Still, having her along made any tête-à-tête with Holly even less likely. He didn't know if he would be more likely to accuse her or forgive her if they were alone—nor was he sure yet which he ought to do.

Outdoors, the three teams headed in different directions. William eagerly led his team towards the orchard, where he claimed he had found an enormous bunch of mistletoe the year before.

"Hold up, hold up, we have ladies with us," Hunt admonished him. He paused, looking back at Holly and Camilla toiling through the snow. Already it appeared that his stepmother was regretting her decision to come. And Holly looked pale, he thought. Instinctively, he held out his arm for her. Camilla hurried forward, taking the proffered arm before Holly could.

"Oh, thank you, dear boy. I fear I am not at all accustomed to walking through snow." Behind her, Holly gave him a half smile and shrugged. "Now where has that little monkey William got to?" the duchess continued.

"I'll go ahead with him, ma'am," said Holly, quickening her pace.

"Very well, my dear. I am not certain I can manage without Hunt's support."

Hunt glanced down at Camilla impatiently, wondering why she had chosen to come along at all. As she trotted past, Holly smiled and Hunt felt a tug at his heart. He smiled back.

"My! How pretty the estate looks, covered in snow," commented Camilla, slowing her pace further. She chattered on, walking more and more slowly, until William and Holly were completely out of sight. "So much nicer than the rain and sleet they get farther south, don't you agree?"

"I suppose so," replied Hunt distractedly. "Though Holly told me once that it snows often enough in Derbyshire to preclude hunting for at least a part of every winter."

"Does it, indeed? I had thought—" She broke off at the sound of a shrill childish scream somewhere ahead.

"That sounds like William!" Leaving the duchess where she stood, Hunt raced towards the rise. As he ran, he heard other cries that sounded like Holly's. He forced himself faster through the snow, knee-deep in places.

Topping the rise, he saw a sight that made his heart stand still. Below was the pond he and Anne had mentioned at dinner last night—the pond Anne had fallen into as a child. Now it was William who had fallen through the ice, still thin after only a few days of frost.

Holly was in the water, too, apparently attempting to wade out to where William floundered, a few yards away. As he watched, she lost her footing and fell forward, for a moment disappearing completely under the water. Then she was up again, half-walking, half-swimming towards the child.

"Hold on!" shouted Hunt. "I'm coming!"

CHAPTER FIFTEEN

As the ice water closed over her head, Holly almost panicked. Then, desperately, she remembered the swimming lessons Noel had given her when they were eleven, and began to stroke with her hands against the water. In seconds, though it seemed far longer, she broke through the surface into the wintry daylight.

William was nearly within reach, his face white and scared, his arms flailing wildly. Holly righted herself. Yes, her feet could still touch the bottom.

"William, listen to me!" she shouted authoritatively. It would never do to let the child know she was nearly as frightened as he. "Stop thrashing about and reach for my hand."

Holly reached as far forward as her arm would stretch, using the other against the water to maintain her balance on the slippery ooze on the bottom of the pond. Slowing the windmill action of his limbs, William finally focused on her.

"Everything will be all right," she assured him as calmly as she could through her chattering teeth. "Just take my hand."

A little of the fear went out of the boy's eyes and he stretched one mittened hand towards her. As soon as he stopped thrashing, however, he sank like a stone.

Holly made a grab for him, but he was still a few inches out of reach. Dimly, she heard shouting behind her, but she did not dare turn to look. Pushing her feet against the mud, she propelled herself forward. She could still see William just below the surface, and in a moment she had him under the arms, lifting his head above the water.

The frightened child immediately seized her in a death grip, nearly pulling them both under. Making soothing noises, Holly turned back to the edge of the pond. The snowy shore looked impossibly far away, though in fact it was only a few yards. Her whole body was racked by such violent shivers that she could scarcely stand.

Then, to her overwhelming relief, she saw Hunt. Behind him, and off to one side, Sir Philip was also running towards them, followed more distantly by Lady Anne.

"Stay where you are, Holly! I'll get you both!" shouted Hunt, peeling off his caped cloak.

Gratefully, Holly halted, clasping the now-sobbing William to her chest.

"Wait!" cried Sir Philip, coming up just then. "Take my hand, Hunt, and we'll form a chain to pull them back."

Hunt nodded. Sir Philip remained with one foot on shore while Hunt waded out to where Holly stood. She inched forward, and in a moment Hunt reached her outstretched hand. Their progress back was slow, for William's weight impeded Holly's movement. As soon as he could, Hunt took the boy from her and handed him to his father. Then, one arm firmly around Holly's shoulders, he guided her back onto the snowy shore.

By now, everyone else in the party had gathered around the pond, brought by William's screams when the ice first cracked. Lady Anne wept over William, still in her husband's arms, while the other children looked on with frightened expressions.

"Is he going to die, Mother?" asked Alice, her lower lip trembling.

Quickly, Anne pulled herself together. "Of course not, darling, but we must get him back to the house at once and into a hot bath. Reggie, dear, will you run ahead and have one drawn?''

Lord Reginald pelted off towards the house and Sir Philip headed after him as quickly as he could manage. The duke and duchess followed with the other children. Anne started to join them, but then stopped and turned to Holly.

"There is no way I can ever thank you enough. You saved my son's life." Heedless of Hunt, who by now was nearly supporting Holly's whole weight, she hugged her sister-in-law fiercely.

"Why, you are nigh frozen to death! Hunt, you must get her into a bath immediately—and yourself, too. We'll talk more later, my dear." With that, she turned and ran after her husband.

"Th-th-thank you," Holly managed to stammer as Hunt propelled her up the hill towards the house. "I d-don't—"

"Don't try to talk now," he said shortly. "Walk as quickly as you can. It will warm you somewhat."

Holly bit her lip, though it was so numb that she could not feel her teeth against it. With the others nowhere near, Hunt plainly saw no need for tenderness, or even civility. The affection she had imagined in his eyes earlier had been an illusion, after all.

Sudden tears that sprang as much from disappointment as from reaction to her recent ordeal blinded Holly and in a moment she was sobbing uncontrollably. With a muffled oath, Hunt lifted her in his arms as though she weighed no more than William and bore her swiftly to the house.

THE NEXT FEW HOURS were hazy for Holly. Someone, she was not sure who except that it was not Hunt, stripped her of her sodden, icy clothing and deposited her in a steaming bath. As she slowly thawed, her mind seemed to grow foggier rather than clearer.

She did not remember getting out of the tub at all. She was dried, wrapped in a warm, dry flannel nightgown and tucked beneath several layers of blankets with a hot brick at her feet. Then she sank into blissful oblivion.

When she awoke, Lady Anne was at her bedside, just seating herself in the chair.

"Oh, I did not mean to wake you, Holly," she said contritely. "I've just seen William to sleep again and wanted to sit with you for a while. How are you feeling?"

"Warm again." Holly smiled at Anne's anxious expression, trying to reassure her. "Only a bit achy. Probably because I have not been used to so much exercise. I shall be fine, I am certain."

Anne breathed a sigh of relief. "I wished to thank you again for what you did. 'Twas very brave. I daren't think of what would have happened had you not been by when William fell in." She shuddered.

"I'm very glad I was near enough to be of use. Still, if I had stayed even closer to him, it would not have happened at all."

"Nonsense!" said Anne roundly. "William has already told me that you warned him to stay off of the ice but that he would not listen. I know from long experience how difficult it is to keep that boy from a course once he is set on it. Had I been with him, he'd have done just the same, I am sure. And I cannot swim. I really have great cause to be thankful that you were there instead of I."

Holly managed a wan smile but said nothing, feeling illogically as though she had betrayed Hunt's trust yet again.

Anne went on, "In fact, in William's eyes, as well as my own, you are quite a heroine. All through his bath he could talk of nothing else."

Holly wished she dared ask whether Hunt shared his nephew's opinion, but she could not. Still, Anne's words comforted her somewhat.

"I am only glad that William is all right. He has suffered no ill effects, then?"

"None at all. 'Twill give him something to boast of to the other lads when we return home." Anne laid one hand on Holly's forehead. "I am relieved that you are not feverish, either. Grandmama wished to have the doctor in to see both of you, but the duchess pooh-poohed the suggestion. For once, it appears that Camilla may be in the right."

Holly frowned. "Are you not close to the duchess, either?" She surprised herself with the question, which was undoubtedly impertinent. Her recent experience had apparently not made her any more cautious.

But Anne answered readily enough, after a quick glance towards the open doorway. "I fear that neither Hunt nor I have ever really regarded Camilla as a mother—nor has she encouraged it. 'Twas not so hard on me, for I was too young to remember my real mother and Grandmama did her best to fill her place. But for Hunt it was difficult."

"How so?" prompted Holly. She so desperately needed to understand what drove her husband.

"Well, Papa seemed to have little time for him—or the estates—after he married Camilla. As a result, Hunt took on responsibilities that should not by rights have been his for years. By the time he was twelve he was practically managing all of Wickburn, with Grandmama's help. Even now, he takes tasks on himself that most men would leave to their stewards."

"Yes, I had noticed that," said Holly. "Both he and Grandmama appear to have a very strong sense of responsibility to the land and the people here."

"Oh, between them I doubt there are any tenants in England with less to complain of. But sometimes I think Hunt pushes himself too hard."

Holly had to agree, remembering the inordinate amount of travel he'd had to do on Foreign Office business. And look at the thanks he had received.

"He will not listen to me, Holly, but perhaps you might have some influence on him," Anne suggested. "Help him to take life a little less seriously."

First Grandmama and now Anne, thought Holly in exasperation. In fact that was precisely what she had tried to do at the start of their marriage—a task she had been making some progress at before everything fell apart. Aloud she said, "I will do my best."

Anne smiled and stood. "Of course. How presumptuous you must think me! But I daresay you would be the same were it your brother. You rest now, and I will return to speak with you in the morning."

"How is she?" asked Hunt when Anne peeked into the library, where he sat alone. "Is she awake?"

"Yes, but I told her to rest. You should rest, too, Hunt. You were nearly as chilled as she, and you've done little but sit by her bed since getting out of your own bath."

"I'm fine." He dismissed her concern brusquely. "I was not in the water for more than a moment."

And if he were ill, he thought, it would be no more than he deserved. He had allowed, even encouraged, Holly to go ahead with William so that he need not deal with his feelings for her. His misguided pride had nearly cost them all dearly.

"Hunt, it wasn't your fault, either," said Anne gently, sitting down next to him.

He looked up, startled. "What do you mean?" Like his grandmother, Anne sometimes seemed to have an uncanny ability to read his mind.

"Both you and Holly seem determined to blame yourselves for what happened. As I told her, William has been getting into scrapes since he was a baby. He eluded the vigilance of his nurse time without number, and she is the most trustworthy soul in the world. And now his tutor complains to me constantly of how difficult he is to control."

"Rather like me at that age, eh?" Hunt allowed himself a reluctant smile.

"Yes, rather like you—before you began taking the cares of the world on your shoulders, at least." Anne's smile held something of concern, but Hunt looked away.

"Still, I should not have allowed the two of them to go on ahead like that. Holly is not as familiar—"

"Now there you go again." Anne cut him off. "Holly is a grown woman, and an intelligent one. I doubt she would thank you for treating her like a child. Pamper her when she needs it, yes, but do not try to do her thinking for her. She's perfectly capable of taking responsibility for her own actions." She rose. "Now, if you will excuse me, I would like to look in on William one more time."

Hunt sat there after she left, staring into the fire. Was that what he had been doing all along—treating Holly like a child?

Certainly, he had ordered most of the details of their lives, even to include the decorating of her own rooms. But that was what husbands did, wasn't it? He recalled her eagerness to be involved in Foreign Office affairs—and how he had forbidden it.

He had never shown even a modicum of trust in her judgement, he realized. Instead of making her a partner in his life, he had treated her more like a possession or, yes, like a child—to be instructed by his grandmother and guided by himself. Small wonder if she wanted more from life.

Hunt now remembered his intention of living apart from Holly after the Christmas season was over—and recoiled from it. The moment he'd seen her in danger, the truth had struck him again with blinding clarity.

He loved her.

No matter what she had done, no matter what her feelings towards him, he loved her. What was more, he needed her—needed her far more than she could possibly need him, improbable though that would have seemed to him mere days ago. He could not imagine his life without her.

But—supposing *she* wished to part from *him?* Could he bear to let her go, after coming so close to losing her this morning?

Hunt stood and walked over to the window, where he stared out across the bleak, dead landscape. It must be her decision. If she wanted to leave, he would have to let her, though it killed him. It was as Anne said—she was a grown woman, not a child, not his possession.

But before he gave her that choice, he would do everything in his power to win her love.

HOLLY WAS MORE than a little disgusted at herself when she found she was still weak the next morning. It was not as though she had been injured, she told herself. A fright and a dunking in ice water should not still be affecting her so a day later.

Determinedly, she sat up when a maid came in with her breakfast tray. She would never clear things up with Hunt if she spent her time at Wickburn playing the invalid. When she tried to stand, however, her head swam and she had to sit back down.

"Holly, dear, pray don't overexert yourself," exclaimed Lady Anne, following her breakfast into the room. She nodded for the maid to leave them, and when she was gone, said, "If Camilla were in your place, she would expect cosseting for a fortnight at the very least, I assure you. It will do you no harm in *her* eyes to pretend to a greater degree of, ah, delicacy than you truly feel."

"My sister Blanche is the same." Holly chuckled at Anne's wry smile. "She always made me feel that good health was somehow less than ladylike."

"Then you know exactly what I mean. Camilla has done the same to me for most of my life." Anne rolled her eyes.

"'How excessively *strong* you are, my dear,'" she mimicked.

Holly sighed. "I fear this time my, ah, delicacy is not completely feigned. But I cannot imagine why I should still feel as weak as dishwater. It is most frustrating, I assure you, when there is so much to do before Christmas."

"You will feel more the thing by tomorrow, I am sure." Anne picked up the breakfast tray where the maid had left it and brought it forward. "You ate very little yesterday. Perhaps that is much of the problem."

Unfortunately, Holly found the sight of poached eggs and toast far from appealing. When the odour of what was probably an excellent breakfast reached her nostrils, her stomach gave an alarming lurch.

"Oh, no! Please, take it away," she begged. Anne obliged quickly, setting the tray back on the dressing-table. "I'm sorry," Holly said lamely when she turned back to face her. "I—I seem to have little appetite lately."

"Lately?" Anne's bright eyes regarded her searchingly. "Then your appetite has been off since before yesterday's accident?"

Holly nodded. "For a week or two, actually. I expect it is the result of my worry over Hunt's arrest and the excitement of his release."

Anne's eyes did not leave her face, though she started to smile. "Tell me, is it primarily in the mornings that the idea of eating is repugnant to you?"

"Why... why, yes, I suppose it is. Why?" She could not imagine what Anne found so amusing about her queasiness.

"Pardon me if I am impertinent, Holly. You would probably prefer discussing such matters with your own mother, but as she is not here..."

"What matters?" Holly was genuinely confused now. "What are you talking about?"

Anne pursed her lips for a moment, then appeared to come to some sort of decision. "Pray excuse me for asking, dear, but how long has it been since you had your monthly courses?"

Holly blinked. "I—I'm not sure. Quite some time—before I left London, in fact—oh! You cannot think... ?"

Her sister-in-law nodded. "I think it very likely, actually. 'Twould also account for why your experience yesterday still has you feeling so weak. Come now! 'Tis nothing to blush over. I should think you would be delighted—I know Hunt will be!" She was beaming now.

"Oh, no! You must not tell him." Holly reached out and put a hand on her arm. At the surprised query in Anne's eyes, she stammered, "I—I wish to tell him myself, please. But... not just yet."

"Not... ? Oh, I see! You wish to surprise him. What a wonderful Christmas present, to be sure!"

"Yes! Yes, that's it," Holly agreed in relief. She recalled Hunt's words on her first night back at Wickburn. *"The sooner we get an heir, the sooner we can part...."* If Hunt knew she was with child, he might never come near her again.

"Still, under the circumstances, I think perhaps we ought to have Dr. Collins out to examine you. A shock such as you had yesterday cannot have been good for the babe."

"No, really, I do not think that is necessary," said Holly, forcing a smile. "I feel quite well, only a trifle weak. And if the doctor came, surely he would tell Hunt how matters stand. I do so want it to be a surprise." She hated to deceive Anne, who had shown herself a true friend and more of a sister than Blanche had ever been, but she could see no other choice.

"Very well then," said Anne doubtfully. "But if you become feverish, or start to feel really ill, we must send for him at once."

"Of course," Holly agreed. But she was determined that would not become necessary. First, she had to tell Hunt the truth about Teasdale, and about her own stupidity. Then, she had to discover whether there was any chance that she could win his affection. And she had to do it by Christmas. She could come up with no plausible excuse to keep her secret longer than that.

"I can scarcely wait to see Hunt's face when you tell him," Anne was saying. "What a marvellous Christmas this will be!"

"I hope so," said Holly, half to herself. "I certainly hope so."

To HOLLY'S SURPRISE, Hunt came to her room twice that day, both times to ask so solicitously after her health that she began to wonder whether Anne had told him of her condition, after all. On both occasions he was accompanied by his grandmother and once by Camilla, as well, so there was no opportunity for private conversation. Still, she found it immeasurably pleasant to hear his voice, almost tender now, instead of angry or cold.

By the following afternoon, she was getting restless. Anne had forbidden her to rise that morning, even though she felt perfectly strong.

"You will indulge me in this, Holly, if you wish me to keep your secret until Saturday. We must subject your precious burden to no further danger."

With that Holly could scarcely argue, and she had no doubt that Anne would fulfil her threat if she disobeyed. "I believe you quite enjoy playing the tyrant," she told her sister-in-law accusingly.

"I have had so few chances, you see, except with the children," Anne laughingly agreed. "If Grandmama knew the truth, she'd be in here with reams of advice, so consider yourself fortunate."

"I'll hear it all after Christmas, I imagine." But Holly was smiling now. Grandmama, at least, would be overjoyed by her news, and it pleased her to know she could thereby repay a measure of the old woman's invaluable help and friendship.

As the hours crept by, Holly had an inkling of the frustration Hunt must have felt during his weeks in prison. She could not despair, however—the knowledge that she carried Hunt's child was too precious, too joyous to allow that. This child, she was determined, would not grow up a stranger to one of its parents. It was absolutely essential now that she mend her fences with her husband, not only for her own sake and his, but in order to provide a loving family for their child.

And Noel—Noel would be an uncle! Her brother, she was certain, would be delighted to hear that. But to hear it, he had to return safely to England. Somehow, she had to convince Hunt that Noel was no traitor. And if she could not... Slowly, painfully, she realized that she would still have to tell Hunt the truth. As deeply as she cared for Noel, Hunt had first claim on her loyalty—and her love. She would keep no further secrets from him.

Hunt needed her, she was now convinced, nearly as much as she needed him. Once she made a full confession, she would do her best to win him over. Then, on Christmas, she would tell him about their child, as she had promised Anne. If he still wished to be rid of her—she swallowed hard at the thought—then she would not oppose him. She loved him too much to make his life miserable by staying.

CHAPTER SIXTEEN

THE NEXT MORNING Holly was up and half dressed before Mabel made her appearance.

"I am happy to see you are feeling better, my lady," said her abigail, hurrying forward to do up the buttons at her back.

When a maid brought her breakfast tray, she told her to take it away. "I will breakfast with the family today."

Lady Anne, coming in at that moment, heard her. "I suppose it would be fruitless to urge you to stay abed one more day?"

"Completely," Holly assured her. "Yesterday was one day too long, in fact. Another would drive me mad, I'm certain. In any event, is not the Christmas Ball set for tonight? The duchess would not thank me for missing that, I think."

"You do not intend to dance, surely?" asked Anne worriedly.

But Hunt, just leaving his own chamber, said from behind her, "And why should she not? I should think three days in bed would have her quite recovered by now."

Anne started, and said rather lamely, "I, ah, simply would not wish her to overdo, and perhaps, ah, precipitate a fever."

"Nonsense! Holly is not a hothouse flower like Camilla, Annie. Pray do not try to make her into one." He turned his gaze to his wife, and smiled.

Holly felt her heart leap at his look, but only said, "Thank you, my lord. I am glad you are here to overrule my jailer. I feel perfectly well, as I told her yesterday." Too late, she realized that the word "jailer" was ill-chosen, but Hunt did not appear to notice.

"If you are ready then, my dear, may I escort you down to breakfast?" He held out an arm to her, his expression almost as warm as it had been in the days before all the trouble had begun.

"Of course." Almost afraid to believe she was not dreaming, Holly stood, oblivious to Mabel's attempts to put one last pin in her hair, and placed her hand on his elbow.

Anne still regarded her disapprovingly, but Holly only smiled brightly at her. Her sister-in-law could not know what a momentous occasion this was. Her heart lighter than it had been in months, Holly accompanied her husband downstairs.

She saw at once that while she had been confined to bed, the rest of the family had outdone themselves with the Christmas decorations. Even more greenery was festooned about the Great Hall than there had been for her wedding day. Mistletoe, in particular, was in astonishing profusion. As she descended the staircase, she counted no fewer than six kissing boughs.

"Was William allowed to go back out to hunt mistletoe?" she asked in surprise.

"Yes, yesterday," replied Hunt with a chuckle. "He pestered Annie until she gave in, then made up for lost time, as you can see."

"I should have been more recalcitrant, then. Perhaps she'd have allowed me out of bed, as well." She could not take offence at Anne's concern, though, considering the cause.

"Annie has grown quite fond of you," said Hunt with an enigmatic smile. "I can't fault her for taking a bit of extra care. Can you?"

Holly shook her head. "I've never been one to hold a grudge, at any rate." She tried to infuse her words with extra meaning, and for a moment imagined she saw a flicker of comprehension in Hunt's eyes.

He looked away and cleared his throat. "Do you really feel up to attending the ball tonight? Don't hesitate to tell me, or Annie, if you become fatigued. We care about your health, you know."

Hunt knew it was cowardly to couple his sentiments with Anne's, to hide behind her, as it were, but he was not yet ready to voice his feelings plainly. First he must gauge his wife's.

Had she been accusing him of holding a grudge just now, or was she subtly telling him that she was willing to forgive his accusations and foul temper, his jealousy—even his arrogant management of her life? The first was certainly true, and not entirely without cause, but he took hope from the second possibility.

"Thank you," Holly said. "But I feel perfectly fine, as I told you. I am quite looking forward to the ball, in fact, after three days of idleness."

Her shy smile went right to his heart. In that instant, he forgave her everything, whatever she had done. If she was willing to start anew, then so was he.

"Might I claim the honour of the first dance, then?" he asked with mock formality to conceal the emotion that welled up within him—an emotion he had spent months denying, and which now nearly drowned him in its intensity.

"Of course, my lord," replied Holly with a charming dimple, dropping him a half curtsy. "I shall look forward to it."

HOLLY DRESSED with painstaking care for the Christmas Ball, telling herself that this could well be the most important night of her life. Deliberately, she chose a gown similar to the one she had worn the night she and Hunt first met. He probably wouldn't remember, but it would be a reminder to her of what she hoped to accomplish.

"No, Mabel, not the ribbon. Use these flowers in my hair instead."

"But my lady, the ribbon was meant to go with the dress. See, it is precisely the same shade of crimson—" Her abigail held it against the ribbons threaded through the bodice of the white gauze-over-satin gown.

"Never mind that. I prefer flowers in my hair tonight." She had worn this same spray of artificial white flowers the night she and Hunt met, and had kept them ever since, safe in her ribbon box. They still looked almost new.

Mabel blinked at her mistress's firm tone and silently replaced the crimson ribbon in the box.

A few minutes later, a tap came at her door. Taking a deep breath to steady herself, Holly motioned Mabel to open it.

Hunt almost looked his old self, she thought, except for a depth, an awareness, in his eyes that she did not remember from before their marriage. But then she suspected that the past year had wrought its changes on her, as well.

A sapphire embedded in his snowy cravat reflected the deep blue of his coat, and for a moment Holly wondered if he, too, had deliberately dressed similarly to the night they had met. Then, smiling at herself, she dismissed the fancy. Blue had always been Hunt's preferred colour, and she had seen him dressed in it time without number. There was nothing remarkable in it, surely.

"The rest of the family is already below, I believe," he said, a faint glimmer of a twinkle in his eyes echoing her welcoming smile. "Shall we join them?"

The first guests were just arriving as Hunt and Holly reached the foot of the grand staircase. An orchestra had been installed on the dais at the far end of the Great Hall and all the furniture had either been removed or lined against the walls and in alcoves. The chandeliers and sconces blazed with candlelight, making the enormous room nearly as bright as day.

"Holly, *darling*," gushed the duchess, taking her arm to guide her to her place near the entrance. "I told Wickburn there was no need to fear you would be unequal to my ball. You have always been so excessively strong."

Recalling Lady Anne's mimicry two days before, Holly was hard pressed to keep her lips from twitching, especially when she caught her sister-in-law's eye from the other side of the doorway. "Why thank you, your grace," she said evenly, and had the satisfaction of seeing Anne engage in a fit of coughing.

Further conversation was thankfully impossible for the next half-hour or so, as people arrived in a steady stream, and Holly and Anne both had a chance to regain their equilibrium. Then, the orchestra struck up the first dance.

"I must deprive you of one of your greeters, ma'am," said Hunt to his stepmother. "My wife and I are engaged for this set."

The duchess pouted slightly. "I had rather hoped you might dance the first with me. After all, I arranged this ball to recognize your return to us, Hunt."

"Not officially, I hope, as Father did such a superb job of keeping everything quiet in London. At any rate, Holly deserves equal recognition, for her heroics on Monday." He slanted a smile down at Holly that made her heart race.

The duke stepped forward at once. "Allow me, then, my dear," he said with a bow.

"You may claim your dance later, Father. My wife is promised to me for this dance. You and Camilla must join us to open the ball." He did not wait for further argument, but took Holly by the hand to lead her out onto the floor. The other guests took their cue from him, and in a moment the hall was alive with bright, swirling couples.

At the end of the set, they found themselves near the archway leading into the supper-room. Hunt gazed down at her. "Shall we escape the crush for a moment? You mustn't overexert yourself all at once, after all."

Holly smiled her agreement, though she felt as healthy as she had ever been. Taking her husband's arm, she accompanied him through the partially curtained arch.

"My enterprising nephew did not limit his decorations to the Hall, I see," Hunt commented, glancing upwards. Holly followed his gaze to see the enormous kissing bough suspended directly above them. "Never let it be said that I am one to flout time-honoured traditions," he said, lowering his lips to hers.

Holly had been longing for his kiss for so long that the first touch came almost as a shock. Pleasure far beyond anything she had anticipated flowed through her. What had begun as a quick, teasing kiss rapidly developed into something far wilder and more significant. He pulled her closer, exploring her mouth with his tongue.

She responded eagerly, hungrily, but after a moment he drew back, putting her gently away. Belatedly mindful that someone might come through the arch at any moment, she dropped her hands from where they had strayed about his neck and nervously smoothed her skirts. She did not quite dare to meet his eyes.

Hunt cleared his throat. "I, ah, suppose we should return to the Hall. Are you not engaged to my father for the next set?" He sounded as embarrassed as she suddenly felt.

She nodded, torn between happiness and uncertainty. Plainly he still desired her. But was desire alone enough to make him overlook what she had done? She would find out soon. Before she slept this night she would tell him the truth—all of it.

DESPITE HER NERVOUSNESS over the upcoming confession, Holly enjoyed the next few hours. Unlike the ball where she and Hunt had met, they were not restricted to two dances together and he claimed her for nearly all of them. Even when she left his side to dance with others, her euphoria held, making her laugh at her father-in-law's sallies as she had not done since the days immediately following her wedding.

"Heroics seem to have done you good, my dear," commented Wickburn as their second dance drew to a close.

"Or perhaps it was the dousing in ice water. If other ladies knew what a sparkle it puts in one's eyes, we'd have them dunking themselves in droves."

Holly laughed merrily at his silliness as she twirled into the final turn of the dance. But then her eye was caught by a young man hovering near the curtain separating the Great Hall from the supper-room.

"Noel?" she gasped.

"What was that?" asked the duke as she turned back to face him for the bows.

"Oh, nothing," replied Holly shakily. "If... if you will excuse me, your grace—" Scarcely waiting for his response, she made her way through the crowd towards the spot where she had seen the man who looked so much like her brother.

When she reached the curtain no one was there, and as she peered frantically around, her mind finally began to function again.

Of course it could not have been Noel. Now that she thought on it, the man had been dressed as a servant—most likely one of the villagers that Grandmama had specially hired for the occasion.

Surely, though, she would remember any man who so resembled Noel, even if she had only met him once. And she had met most of the villagers several times.

There was only one door leading out of the supper-room. Without pausing to consider the possible consequences, Holly went through it. A narrow stairway led down to the kitchens below, where a bustle of preparation for the midnight supper was under way. The aroma of roasting meats and baking bread drifted up to her, along with the clatter of pots and pans.

Cautiously, Holly descended the staircase and peeped into the huge kitchen. None of the busy servants bore any resemblance to Noel. Beside her, though, was the door leading out into the kitchen gardens—perhaps he had gone that way. Silently, she turned the handle and let herself out into the wintry night.

HUNT WAS FINDING the evening a sweet torment. Desires he had worked ruthlessly to subdue in recent days were alive and raging within him, resurrected in an instant by that kiss. And she had responded to him. Awareness of that, and of her, burned more fiercely with each touch, even each glimpse of his wife. His wife. The very phrase seemed imbued with a lush sensuality he had never attributed to it before.

Before the start of the ball, he had noticed how very much she looked as she had the night they first met. Her dress could not be the same one, of course, but it was hauntingly similar, even down to the spray of flowers in her hair. His feelings for her now were far stronger, however, than they had been that first night. Now he was truly in love, rather than merely infatuated, as he had been then.

The dance ended. Hunt made his bows to his partner, whose name he could not even recall, and turned eagerly to locate Holly for the next one. Ah! There she was, by the supper-room. Perhaps he could catch her under the mistletoe again before their set began.

As he hurried forward, she disappeared behind the curtain. Did she have the same thought in mind? His heart raced as he smiled to himself. The little minx!

But when he entered the supper-room, Holly was not standing beneath the kissing bough as he had expected. Looking around the room in confusion, he saw the door leading down to the kitchens just closing. Had Camilla or Grandmama sent her on some errand?

Hunt nearly turned back to the ballroom to await her return, but then, on impulse, decided to follow her. She might need help up the stairs, he reasoned to himself, what with this being her first day up after her accident.

The cooks and maids looked up curiously from their work when he strode into the kitchen and he paused. Holly was not there. Had it not been she who had gone through the door, after all? But then, where the devil had she got to? Nodding curtly, he turned back to the stairs, only then noticing the door at their foot.

Feeling more than a little foolish by now, he opened it and stepped out into the kitchen gardens. Surely Holly would have had no reason to come out here! With his hand still on the door handle, he glanced quickly around, intending to go back upstairs and look for Holly there.

He froze in shock. There, not ten paces from him, was his wife—firmly clasped in the arms of another man!

"What the devil is going on?" he exploded, anger and pain warring within him. He had come so close to convincing himself that she cared!

The couple broke apart to stare at him and Hunt noted with an odd sense of detachment that the man was dressed as a servant—and was completely unknown to him. He had thought he could forgive her anything, but—

Holly came towards him at once. "Oh, Hunt," she said, her voice quavering with an emotion he could not identify, "'tis Noel! He has returned, safe at last!"

"Noel?" Hunt turned to glower at the stranger.

"My brother—you have heard me speak of him, Hunt! He has been in France this past year and more, gathering information. It was he who was writing to me, whose letter you caught me burning last May, whose letter...sent you to prison."

"Your brother?" Hunt felt dazed, so unexpected was this twist. "But your brother is in Upper Canada," he said stupidly.

The young man spoke now. "No. That is the story we put about so that no questions would be asked about my absence. Only Holly knew the truth." He extended his hand. "I am delighted to make your acquaintance at last, my lord."

Hunt automatically shook his hand, though he was thinking hard now. "Noel Paxton? I recall no agent by that name. Did you use an alias?"

"He . . . he was not sent by the War Office," said Holly before he could answer. "But he *was* working for England . . . were you not, Noel?" She turned back to her brother anxiously. They'd had no chance yet to talk, but surely, if he was here—

"Of course, silly girl. How can you ask?" He glanced at Hunt. "You may know me as 'Puss in Boots.' 'Tis the way I signed my reports."

"Puss in Boots?" repeated Hunt. "*The* Puss in Boots?"

"Of course!" Holly exclaimed excitedly. "Why did I not make the connection before? That was ever your favourite fairy tale when we were young."

Noel grinned. "I suppose there is no harm now in admitting it, as I am unlike to resume my role now that peace negotiations are under way. Paris will fall before spring, Vandover, you mark my words."

This appeared to divert Hunt's attention. "Before spring, say you?" he asked. "Then you must have discovered—"

Impatiently, Holly interrupted them before they could begin a political discussion. "But what brings you here now, Noel, tonight?"

He turned back to her. "You, of course. I left Paris as soon as word reached me that one of my letters had been intercepted," he said. "I was in a cold sweat imagining what might happen to you because of it, I can tell you, Holly."

Noel had been safely away from France all this time! She could scarcely credit it. "'Twas not I who was in danger, but Hunt," she told him, glancing up at her husband.

Noel followed her gaze and smiled crookedly. "Yes, I heard what happened when I reached London. I must apologize most profoundly for the indignity you bore for my sake and my sister's, my lord. And I must thank you. When I first heard of Holly's marriage I was sure no man could be worthy of her, but it would seem she chose wisely, indeed. I am in your debt." He swept Hunt an elegant bow that was at odds with his attire.

"If you are indeed the elusive Puss in Boots, then I have reason to thank you, as well," replied Hunt. "Certain information you sent us was instrumental in the capture of more than one French spy."

"Teasdale has been caught, then? Why did you not tell me?" Holly demanded.

Hunt turned back to her with a frown. "Teasdale? What do you mean?"

But Noel was already answering. "Yes, Teasdale has been apprehended. Someone notified the authorities at Plymouth and they arrested him when he tried to take ship for South America. The news reached London even as I did."

"I was that someone!" she exclaimed. "I was determined he should not escape after everything he had done to me—and to Hunt. And of course he murdered poor Lord Meecham, as well."

"Will one of you kindly tell me what you are talking about?" Hunt demanded.

"Teasdale was the traitor you were seeking," Holly explained. "The one giving Foreign Office information to the French."

"Are you certain of this?"

She nodded. "Noel told me that it was a clerk, one who had joined the Foreign Office since the first of the year. Teasdale was the only one who fit that description. Besides, he admitted it to me."

Hunt looked questioningly at Noel. "Why did you send us nothing about this?"

"I thought I had." Noel's expression was grim when he turned to Holly. "I made it perfectly clear in that letter that you were to tell your husband, and leave the investigation to him. Plainly you did not." Both men turned to regard her accusingly.

Holly chewed her lip. "Hunt...was away when I received that letter," she said defensively. "I thought if...if

I could prove, on my own, that Teasdale was the traitor, that you would be proud of me, and let me help in other investigations. I never guessed everything would become so...so tangled!''

"Why did you not tell me at once, when I returned?" The gentleness of Hunt's tone made her writhe with shame and embarrassment.

"I fear I did something stupid. You see, before I figured out that the spy was Teasdale, I enlisted his help in trying to discover who the traitor was. He...he persuaded me to give him a list of names—a list I found on your own desk, Hunt—saying that it would help him to narrow the field of suspects." She couldn't bear to look at her husband now, fearing what she might see in his eyes.

She hurried on. "When he found that I knew he was the traitor, he threatened to expose what I had done if I told anyone. He said that it would ruin your career if it came out."

"What list was this?" asked Hunt.

"Something to do with the meetings in Prussia. A list of liaisons, I believe."

Hunt shook his head. "That list was common knowledge. Teasdale could have obtained it for the asking at the Foreign Office. His threat was completely empty."

Holly didn't know whether to laugh or cry. All of those months of misery over nothing! "But he threatened Noel, as well," she said, suddenly remembering. "Teasdale claimed Noel was really working for the French, and that he could have him hanged for it."

"And you believed that of me?" Noel demanded.

"Oh, no, of course not," she said quickly. "But I dared not take the chance." Hunt remained perfectly silent. She risked a quick glance up at him, but his expression told her nothing. "His threats were not completely idle, you know. It was Teasdale who arranged to have you arrested, when I was unable to dissuade you from continuing your investigation. He told me so."

"Teasdale wrote to you in Derbyshire?" Hunt's voice, too, was devoid of expression.

Suddenly aware that her shoulders were bare to the winter night, Holly shivered. "No, I—I came to London, as soon as I heard," she explained. "But before I could convince the duchess to let me see you, he visited Wickburn House. He said he had evidence that would see you hanged if I spoke out against him. He... he would not even allow me to write to you while you were in prison!" she finished plaintively, tears threatening again at remembered anguish over the heartache she must have caused him then.

"You're more gullible than I'd have given you credit for, Holly," said Noel roundly, making her blink. "It ain't as easy as all that to convict a peer of a hanging offence! Teasdale diddled you thoroughly. If you'd told Vandover about him at once, as I told you to, none of this would have happened. He has proven time and again his ability to handle men such as Teasdale."

"He has?" Her tears momentarily forgotten, Holly looked up at Hunt in amazement. He was still inscrutable.

"Did you think the only thing he did on his diplomatic missions was sign papers? He was the Foreign Office's foremost—"

"Never mind that now," said Hunt, interrupting him. "Holly needs to get indoors. She received a severe chill two days since, rescuing my nephew from a frozen pond." His voice was nearly as cold as that water had been, Holly thought, but she couldn't tell whether his anger was directed at her or Noel.

"Will you join us inside?" he continued, icily polite. "There is a ball in progress, and we shall have been missed by now."

"Delighted," said Noel. "That is—" he glanced down at his attire "—if I might change first? I have other clothes in my saddlebags."

"Why *did* you come dressed like that, Noel?" Holly asked through her chattering teeth.

Noel looked rather sheepish. "I just wanted to be certain you were all right before going home to Derbyshire. Some rumours I heard in London... Anyway, I borrowed these from a vastly comely wench whose brother was ill and could not work tonight. But explanations can wait, as Vandover said."

They all trooped up the kitchen stairs to the supper-room, where the midnight supper was already in progress. Their sudden appearance caused quite a commotion.

Reginald was the first to accost them. "We looked high and low for you, brother!"

"Holly, I was worried to death!" exclaimed Lady Anne, coming up just behind him. "Why, your hands are like ice! Hunt, what were you thinking to have her out in the cold all this time?" The duke and the dowager were bearing down on them now, and the duchess had risen from her place with an exclamation.

Quickly, Holly introduced Noel to the family before he made his apologies and went upstairs to change. Hunt then brushed all further questions aside, insisting that Holly have a bit of supper and go early to bed. He made no mention of accompanying her and did not protest when Anne volunteered to take her up.

With a sense of unreality, Holly allowed Mabel to prepare her for bed. She should have felt relieved, she knew. Her confession was over. Teasdale had been apprehended and Hunt and Noel were both safe. There was absolutely nothing left for her to worry about.

Crawling under several layers of quilts, she cried herself to sleep.

CHAPTER SEVENTEEN

HUNT AWOKE EARLY, after a fitful sleep filled with dreams of his time in prison. It was a relief to see the first light of dawn peeping through the window, the blue and gold hangings of his own bedchamber around him.

Then he recalled the events of last night. In spite of his fine resolve to determine how Holly felt about him, to make her love him if she did not already, he had played the coward when the opportunity had presented itself. But she had been so happy, so glowing, at her brother's return that he feared any response to himself might only be an extension of her relief at Noel's return.

And, he rationalized, she had been cold and tired. It was not the time for lengthy declarations or passionate demonstrations. After she had gone up to bed, he and Noel had spent a long time talking. Finally, he believed he understood his wife—understood just how frustrated she must have been by his refusal to include her in his work. He hoped to make it up to her, as far as he was able—if she would give him the chance.

As soon as he was dressed, he went down to the kennels to check on Silverbell. His hounds always settled him, and he hoped that their unconditional affection might give him a measure of the courage he lacked.

"All right, then! Yes, it's I," he called out in response to the eager clamour at his entrance as every hound there vied for his attention. "Hello, Breaker, old fellow. Ho there, Bugle! Let's see how Silverbell is doing, shall we?"

He went around to the whelping pen, where he had been keeping his prize bitch for the past two days.

"Well done, old girl!" he exclaimed at the sight of the squirming brown and black bodies surrounding her. "Let's count them, shall we?" Gently, he lifted each one, checking both gender and conformation as he counted. "Seven! Not a bad night's work, eh, lass?" He patted the hound on the head, and she thumped her tail at the praise.

Behind him, the other hounds began whimpering and yelping again and he turned to find Holly coming through the doorway. At the sight of him she stopped abruptly.

"Oh! I did not know you were here, my lord. I was up early to see Noel off.... He hopes to make Tidebourne by nightfall."

She looked like a winter angel with the white fur trim of her scarlet cloak surrounding her lovely face, mirroring the snowy field behind her. Hunt's heart gave a lurch at the sight, but he beckoned to her.

"I'd planned to give you your birthday present later today, but I suppose now will do, as well."

"My birthday present?" She sounded puzzled. Then she saw the puppies and her face lit up. "Oh, how precious! That is Silverbell, is it not? But—it is December!"

"Yes, I left instructions with Badesly that she was to be bred on her next heat, though I knew it might well come early. She's a prizewinner, you know."

He suddenly felt as awkward as a schoolboy. Perhaps she would laugh, or think he had run mad, giving her a puppy for her birthday instead of a bracelet or a brooch.

Quickly he said, "One of these pups is to be yours—your choice. Saddleback sired them."

"Ooh!" At once she was on her knees in the straw, heedless of her cloak and gown. "For my own?"

She stroked one tiny head, then another. Finally, she looked up at him, and the joy on her face nearly dazzled Hunt, erasing his doubts. No piece of jewellery could possibly have pleased her so.

"You needn't choose now, of course. But I did want to tell you on your birthday. 'Twas most obliging of Silverbell to deliver them in such a timely manner." He thought he must be grinning like a fool.

"Yes, thank you, Silverbell," said Holly, stroking the bitch's head. "And thank *you*, Hunt. This means more to me than you can imagine. I believe it is the best birthday present I have ever received."

Her green eyes glowed and sparkled with unshed tears, though her expression was happy. Suddenly embarrassed, Hunt stood.

"I suppose we had best leave them to their breakfast now, and go to find ours. We can visit them again later."

Holly nodded and allowed him to help her to her feet. As they walked back to the house in silence, Hunt felt amply rewarded. However they had wronged each other in the past, this Christmas would be a new beginning for them.

CHRISTMAS EVE would have been the most perfect day she could imagine had Holly not been gnawed by uncertainty about Hunt's feelings for her. Noel had told her before he left that Hunt had been upset at him, not at her, but she was not sure whether to believe him.

Grandmama and Anne made quite a fuss over her, not allowing her birthday to be completely overshadowed by other Christmas Eve activities. Holly had always regarded those traditions as part of her birthday, however, and entered with enthusiasm into the bringing in of the yule log, the trunk of an entire ash tree, festooned with ivy and holly. Once it was placed in the enormous fireplace at the back of the Great Hall, the duke ceremoniously lit it with a fragment kept from last year's yule log and recited a poem he had composed for the occasion.

Everyone stood around it singing carols while it caught, then proceeded to the dining-room, where all Holly's favourite dishes were featured for dinner, to include apple tart with cream. Even Camilla seemed unusually well disposed towards her that day, with none of the undercurrent of resentment that used to colour her remarks.

The excitement tired Holly, though, and when Lady Anne suggested that she go to bed after tea, she did not resist. Hunt was deep in a discussion with the duke and Sir Philip about Napoléon's anticipated surrender, but when she rose, he stretched and yawned loudly.

"The children will have us up at first light tomorrow, so I believe I will make an early night of it, as well." He offered Holly his arm.

Holly smiled shyly up at him. She had determined to tell Hunt about the child she carried at the first opportunity and this, apparently, would be it. His gift that morning of the puppy had erased most of her doubts, but she still worried that she might have misread his feelings.

"Do you wish me to ring for Mabel for you?" Hunt asked her when they reached the door to her chamber.

Taking a deep breath, Holly shook her head. "Not tonight, I think," she said, echoing his words on their wedding night. The corner of his mouth twitched and she knew he remembered, too.

"But I see that your gown buttons down the back," he said conversationally. "It seems we are faced with a dilemma. Can you think of a solution?"

"Perhaps—" Her voice nearly failed her, and she cleared her throat. "Perhaps you would be kind enough to unfasten them for me?"

"It is the least I can do, I suppose." Hunt's voice was also curiously husky. He opened the door to her room. "I imagine you will need help unpinning your hair, as well?"

Holly looked into his eyes and was trapped there, drowning in deep blue pools. She nodded slowly.

"Turn around, then." He faced her away from him so that he could unbutton her gown.

The moment his eyes no longer held hers, she tried frantically to think. Everything was moving so fast, and she had not yet told him about their child. She had to do it now. She did not really believe that all he had in mind now was begetting an heir, but she had to be certain—absolutely certain. That was the only way.

He had most of the buttons undone now. Softly as a whisper, he placed a kiss just below her ear. Holly closed her eyes and shivered deliciously.

Tell him!

The last button free, he turned her back to face him. His expression was gentle, tender, but there was a flame behind his eyes that kindled an answering spark from deep within her.

Fighting to retain at least an outward appearance of composure, Holly said, "I seem to recall you once saying that you wished for an heir, my lord...."

Hunt's hands abruptly stilled their caressing movements on her arms. "Damnation! Is that what you think I—" He broke off, closing his eyes. The anguish in his expression nearly broke her heart.

When he opened them again, Holly caught her breath at the love she saw reflected there. "I have been such a monster," he said. "All this time you were in pain and I could not see it, could not see anything but my own pride."

"You had every right to doubt me," she said. "I kept secrets from you, something I should never have done. But pray believe me when I say that I have loved you since the day we were married." Hesitantly, she put one hand to his cheek. "Oh Hunt, can you possibly find it in your heart to forgive me?"

"Darling, I forgave you already, when I imagined... well, far worse things. Indeed, I must ask your forgiveness for the doubts I harboured. I should have known you were not capable of such deceit."

Holly smiled ruefully. "I found I was capable of more than my conscience could handle. Oh, Hunt, I missed you so!"

He gathered her into his arms to show her how heartily he echoed that sentiment. At the first touch of their lips, passions too long held in check exploded between them. His mouth still covering hers, Hunt picked Holly up and carried her the few steps to the bed.

Quickly, almost frantically, they stripped off each other's clothing, but with a tenderness that had been lacking in their last passionate joining in London.

"I love you, my beautiful Holly Berry," Hunt whispered before he entered her. The words, even more than his gentle expertise, brought her to a pitch of pleasure she had never experienced before. At last, she felt that she and her husband were truly one.

The next morning, Christmas morning, Holly awoke in her husband's arms, enveloped in a blissful sense of well-being. Half turning, she lovingly explored his face as he slept, looking so peaceful and vulnerable that her heart ached with love for him. As she watched, the thick lashes swept up and his eyes met hers.

Instantly the vulnerability was gone, replaced by strength and awareness, but the peace remained. He looked more at rest than she could ever remember seeing him.

"Have you been watching me long?" he asked, his eyes beginning to twinkle. She had missed that twinkle!

"No, only for a moment. I was thinking how nice it is not to have any secrets for a change. Oh!"

"What? Is there a pin in the bed?"

"I have only just realized, I do have a secret still. I started to tell you last night, but I, ah, forgot."

He chuckled, leaning forward to nuzzle her ear. "What could have distracted you, do you think?"

"'Tis just as well," Holly continued, arching away from him slightly so that she could think. "Now it can be a Christmas present, as I told Anne it would be."

She had his attention now. "A Christmas present? What sort of secret is this, that my sister already knows?"

Suddenly shy, Holly lowered her eyes. "In a way, it was she who told me. Hunt, I believe I am with child."

The look on his face almost made her laugh. "With...? But how...when...?"

"From the night before I left London, I presume. 'Tis the only possibility."

To her amazement, he let out a whoop loud enough to be heard in the servants' quarters and then seized her in a comprehensive hug.

"You have made me the happiest man in the world, Holly! If you only knew how much I've longed—" Suddenly, he began to laugh. "I believe you've topped my gift of a puppy, my love! This is a Christmas for unconventional presents, is it not?"

To Holly's embarrassment, Hunt announced her delicate condition to the others over the breakfast table, where everyone, to include the dowager, was gathered preparatory to leaving for the morning service at the chapel. Everyone agreed that the news was the very thing needed to make it a perfect Christmas.

"I'd been suspecting as much, my dear," the dowager confided, giving Holly a kiss on the cheek. "But I feared it might have been only wishful thinking on my part, so I said nothing."

Even Camilla offered her congratulations with seeming sincerity. "And what happy timing," she added. "If the babe comes in July, as you expect, you will not even have to miss the Season, or perhaps the Little Season, either."

"I am perfectly delighted," declared Reginald. "Especially as Grandmama and I may take some of the credit for this happy resolution."

Hunt and Holly turned curiously to the dowager. "Well, um, yes," she said, looking uncomfortable for the first time since Holly had known her. "When Reggie saw how things were between the two of you last month he came here to Wickburn to consult me about it. Between us, we came up with the little deception about my failing health and final request, to get you both here together. But I must say, it has worked out splendidly!''

"Then you are not ill, after all?'' Holly had thought her happiness had reached its limit, but she was wrong.

"I should have known it,'' said Hunt with mock severity, then kissed his grandmother's cheek. ''You've manipulated me before, Grandmama, but never to better effect. I thank you both.'' He grinned at his brother.

"And I thank you,'' replied Reg. "Now I need never face the horrifying possibility of becoming a duke! You have saved me from a life of dreary responsibility.'' He heaved an exaggerated sigh which made everyone laugh.

Late that afternoon, when the family was all assembled in the parlour prior to Christmas dinner, a knock came on the front door.

"'Twill be some local mummers, I doubt not,'' said the duke as Deeds went to answer it. "I suppose our dinner can wait while we watch their play.'' He led the way into the Great Hall, the others following close behind.

Instead of a group of farmers in disguise, however, a coach stood at the door, from which Noel was helping Holly's mother and sister. With an exclamation of delight, she ran down the steps to greet him.

"'Twas Vandover's idea,'' Noel explained in response to her excited query. "He told me that things had been a bit awkward before but that now you would like to have all the family together for Christmas.''

Holly thanked Hunt with a kiss, then turned to embrace Maman and Blanche. As they accompanied her into the house, she acquainted them with her news. As she had hoped, Maman was ecstatic at the idea of becoming a grandmother and chattered all through dinner about names and toys. Noel, too, was plainly pleased at the idea of becoming an uncle. As for Blanche, she was so overcome by the idea of having a niece or nephew that she finally seemed to forgive Holly for her marriage.

That night they all gathered around the fire in the parlour to hear the dowager read the Christmas story from the enormous family Bible. As Holly sat listening to the words of St. Luke, her head on Hunt's shoulder, with Noel on her other side and her mother and sister seated amicably across from Lady Anne and her husband, she felt that her heart would overflow with happiness.

"'...And the shepherds returned, glorifying and praising God for all the things that they had heard and seen, as it was told unto them,'" concluded the dowager. "I should say we all have a great deal to be thankful for this Christmas, do we not?"

"Indeed we do," said Anne, gazing down at William where he dozed with his head in her lap.

"I know I do," said Noel, with a wink at Hunt and Holly.

"And I," echoed Maman with an adoring look across at Noel.

"I have more to be thankful for than I can express," declared Holly, meeting Hunt's loving gaze.

"I believe I've been more richly blessed than anyone," he said quietly. "A few days ago I nearly lost everything that mattered, and now I have more than I ever dreamed possible. Even my stay in prison was a blessing in disguise, for it showed me that the world will continue spinning without my attention. I believe I'll be willing to take life easier now, perhaps set up my own household."

Holly gasped with delight at his words and he smiled down at her tenderly. Then, in full view of everyone assembled, and without the slightest hint of embarrassment, he bent to kiss her.

A few glorious seconds later, he raised his head to gaze into her eyes. "Of all my many blessings," he said, "what I am most thankful for is you, my Christmas bride."

**Relive the romance...
Harlequin and Silhouette
are proud to present**

by Request™

A program of collections of three complete novels by the most requested authors with the most requested themes. Be sure to look for one volume each month with three complete novels by top name authors.

In January: **WESTERN LOVING**   Susan Fox
                                   JoAnn Ross
                                   Barbara Kaye

Loving a cowboy is easy—taming him isn't!

In February: **LOVER, COME BACK!**   Diana Palmer
                                       Lisa Jackson
                                       Patricia Gardner Evans

It was over so long ago—yet now they're calling, "Lover, Come Back!"

In March: **TEMPERATURE RISING**   JoAnn Ross
                                     Tess Gerritsen
                                     Jacqueline Diamond

Falling in love—just what the doctor ordered!

Available at your favorite retail outlet.

REQ-G3

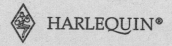

Fifty red-blooded, white-hot, true-blue hunks
from every State in the Union!

Look for MEN MADE IN AMERICA! Written by some
of our most poplar authors, these stories feature fifty of
the strongest, sexiest men, each from a different state in
the union!

Two titles available every other month at your favorite
retail outlet.

In January, look for:

DREAM COME TRUE by Ann Major (Florida)
WAY OF THE WILLOW by Linda Shaw (Georgia)

In March, look for:

TANGLED LIES by Anne Stuart (Hawaii)
ROGUE'S VALLEY by Kathleen Creighton (Idaho)

You won't be able to resist MEN MADE IN AMERICA!

When the only time you have for yourself is...

STOLEN moments ™

Christmas is such a busy time—with shopping, decorating, writing cards, trimming trees, wrapping gifts....

When you do have a few *stolen moments* to call your own, treat yourself to a brand-new *short* novel. Relax with one of our Stocking Stuffers—or with all six!

Each STOLEN MOMENTS title
is a complete and original contemporary romance that's the perfect length for the busy woman of the nineties! Especially at Christmas...

And they make perfect stocking stuffers, too! (For your mother, grandmother, daughters, friends, co-workers, neighbors, aunts, cousins—all the other women in your life!)

Look for the STOLEN MOMENTS display in December

STOCKING STUFFERS:

HIS MISTRESS Carrie Alexander
DANIEL'S DECEPTION Marie DeWitt
SNOW ANGEL Isolde Evans
THE FAMILY MAN Danielle Kelly
THE LONE WOLF Ellen Rogers
MONTANA CHRISTMAS Lynn Russell

HSM2

 **WORLDWIDE LIBRARY**

My Valentine 1994

Celebrate the most romantic day of the year with
MY VALENTINE 1994
a collection of original stories, written by
four of Harlequin's most popular authors...

**MARGOT DALTON
MURIEL JENSEN
MARISA CARROLL
KAREN YOUNG**

*Available in February, wherever
Harlequin Books are sold.*

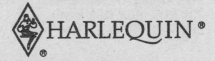

HARLEQUIN®

VAL94